Josh Clark

Accuser

He knows your darkest secrets …

Published by White Feather Press. (www.whitefeatherpress.com)

ISBN 978-1-61808-111-7

Printed in the United States of America

Cover design created by Ron Bell of AdVision Design Group
(www.advisiondesigngroup.com)

White Feather Press

Reaffirming Faith in God, Family, and Country!

For the accused…

Glowing Reviews for Josh Clark

"*Accuser* is a thrilling and thought-provoking depiction of an ancient and continual battle. Josh Clark has penned a powerful story that, from the first page, thrusts readers into a conflict that cuts deeply and personally. Its message lingers long after the final page is read."

–Bill Thomas,
Author of "From the Ashes"
and "The 61st Minute"

"Josh offers us a story of the Father's grace. Our lives truly are held captive until that moment when our heart convinces our mind to accept the love that can be understood only through the nudging of the Holy Spirit. It is at that moment, we are set free. 'While we were yet sinners, Christ died for us.' – Romans 5:8"

Brenda Conley,
Author of "Saving Noelle"

"Josh Clark's latest novel, *Accuser*, is like nothing I've ever read. If you believe in the power of repentance, faith, and redemption, then you will be absolutely blown away by this book."

–R.G. Yoho,
Author of "Death Comes to Redhawk" and "The Evil Day"

"With raw-boned honesty and hard-hitting action, Josh Clark has nailed it! Humanity's deepest fear is revealed – to be found out for who we really are. In *Accuser*, all our sins are enfleshed and come back to haunt us. But, when all hope is lost, we are saved by an ancient grace."

–Skip Coryell,
Author of "The God Virus" and "The Shadow Militia"

Books By Josh Clark

The McGurney Chronicles Series
The Legend of Paul McGurney
Devil's Playground
Infinity
The Ends of the Earth

The Dakota Lester Series
Dakota Divided
Dakota Defined
Dakota Denied

Other Books
Accuser

Part I
Accused

Chapter One

SHE'D HAD NO INKLING THE MAN IN booth thirty-six was dangerous. He had ordered two eggs over-easy, sausage patties and a coffee—black. His eyes were a seawater blue that creased in their corners from at least forty years of smiles. His dark, two-day stubble didn't make him appear disheveled, but rather sexy in a George Clooney or an even vintage Hollywood way. His nose was sharp, his cheekbones high, his lips small and slightly feminine. His fingers were long and thin, and when he had pointed at the breakfast menu, she remembered thinking how precisely manicured his nails were. He wore a blue zip-up hoodie over dark jeans and brown, expensive-looking leather slip-on shoes. She couldn't identify the brand of his shoes, which bothered her, because she knew shoes.

Now, as she huddled behind the waitress station counter, shards of shattered coffee mugs and water glasses all around her, she scolded herself for misinterpreting the one sign of danger:

"Is the restroom near the back exit?" His eyes had smiled, his lips had smiled. He had been so charming, his voice honey-thick with casual sexiness.

"There isn't a back exit. At least not for customers," she had said, ripping his order from her waitress pad. "The men's room is actually the second door on the left down that little hallway." She had pointed to the wall opposite his booth, wondering only briefly how he hadn't managed to figure this out on his own since the women's restroom door and its ridiculous universal placard were visible from his vantage point.

He had smiled and closed his menu with his thin fingers. "Thank you—what is your name again?"

"Sara."

"Thanks, Sara." His smile had widened to reveal two rows of perfectly straight, white teeth. She had been drawn to his smile, not because of its obvious flirtatiousness, but because she could count on her hand how many times an early morning customer had flashed pearly whites. Coffee and teeth were a volatile marriage; from her two years of morning shift experience, breakfast die-hards slurped up the steaming obsidian liquid as diesel fuel for their days, and such a routine caused scummy, stained chompers instead of the variety the man had just flashed. Maybe he had just started drinking the stuff.

Or maybe the coffee, like his civility, had been a ruse.

The diner was eerily silent. Her ears still rang from the first gunshot, and she was fairly certain her palms were imbedded with glass fragments, although the surreal nature of the situation dulled her senses like an anesthetic so she couldn't be sure.

I won't get to Economics on time...

It was a strange thought, one plucked from the thousands that live-streamed through her brain. Her economics class, one of only four classes she had left at Clearton Community College before she transferred to Ohio State the following year, started at ten. Her shift was over at nine-thirty, and the twenty-minute drive to Clearton from Lewiston always left her just enough time to freshen herself up in the bathroom, reapply some lipstick and spritz some perfume to cover the pervading stink of greasy bacon. She had taken the man's order around nine o'clock, and now she waited like the fourteen other diner hostages to see what the man with gun would do next.

"Cell phones!" the man's voice boomed. "Get them out and hold them above your heads. Now!"

Sara readjusted her position so she could extract her iPhone from the right back pocket of her jeans. The heel of her shoe crunched some glass in the process, and she heard the man's shoes turn in her direction.

"You! Out from behind that counter!"

Sara's heartbeat strobed in her temples as she pushed herself across the tile floor. More broken glass crunched underneath her hands and butt as she pressed her body against the waitress station's particle board sides and slowly inched around the protrusion. When she saw the terror-stricken diner patrons with their cell phones over their heads, some of them still seated in their booths with tepid eggs and coffee before them, others huddled in groups of three or four on the floor beside their tables, her breath caught in her throat. This couldn't be happening. It couldn't be real. Things like this happened in movies and thriller novels, not in real life.

It had all happened so quickly...

She had taken the handsome man's order, had shoved her barely-working Bic pen back into her waitress apron. She had been smiling at an elderly couple enjoying matching omelets at table eighteen when the man had pulled the blinds. She had turned to see the George Clooney clone flipping the OPEN sign to CLOSED, had seen him twist the lock on the front door. She had placed his order on the waitress station's countertop, had begun to reach underneath the counter for a water glass. She had known something wasn't right, then, had felt the knot in her stomach as confused diner patrons turned to see why the natural sunlight had been sucked from the room.

"Sir, you can't lock the –" Sara had started. But her words had caught in her throat as the man's hand flashed into his hoodie pouch and produced a handgun. In a millisecond the man's arm had raised, the gun pointed right at her. Survival instincts had taken over, then. She'd heard the gun boom, felt her legs give out from underneath her. As her butt hit the tile floor, shattered glass had rained down upon her. She had barely heard the screams from the diner guests, had barely heard their chairs squeak across the floor as they fell to the ground out of self-preservation.

It had all happened so quickly...

She felt naked and vulnerable as she leaned against the waitress station's side, her entire body now exposed to the diner. The man with the gun stood no more than eight feet away, the gun raised, its barrel pointed at the middle of her forehead. Sara didn't know what unnerved her more: the fact that a loaded gun was pointed directly at her, or that the man's thin lips were pulled into a feral smile.

"Sara! It's good to see you again! Please, show these kind people how to properly slide their cell phones across the floor to where I'm standing." The man's voice dripped with a strange mixture of amicability and scorn. As Sara lowered her phone to the floor and shoved it across the tile toward the man's shoes, she felt repulsed by the fact that she was drawn to his voice. She *knew* his voice—she *knew* it from somewhere, sometime—and it was almost...

...Enticing...

"Nicely done, Sara," the man said. He slowly turned a full circle, the gun sweeping the diner like a deadly Doppler radar. "Everyone, see how Sara did that? Now, it's your turn. Slide your phones to me, please. If anyone tries anything funny in the process, I'll put a bullet through Sara's brain."

He fixed the gun back on her and her heart hammered against her ribcage. The sound of phones sliding across the tile floor filled the small space; and, for a fleeting, hopeful moment, Sara wondered whether Janice, the hefty breakfast cook, had made it out the back door. But when she looked toward the kitchen cutout, she saw Janice leaning against the wall, one hand pressed against her ample chest, sweat pouring from her brow.

She must've been talking to one of the customers when he closed the blinds.

Lewiston was a town just big enough to have a Walmart and a few chain restaurants the neighboring towns didn't, but it was just small enough that everybody knew everybody else. For Janice to leave the kitchen to talk to a customer wasn't uncommon, and Sara wondered what cruel scheme of the universe had damned Janice for being neighborly. Janice was usually cantankerous, uncouth and forgetful; but she knew how to talk to the regulars, and the regulars appreciated her for it. Now, the fifty-something woman's face was turning ashen, and Sara didn't have to be a cardiologist to know Janice was on the verge of a heart attack.

She needs to get out of here...

"Okay, everyone," the man said as he examined the smattering of cell phones scattered at his feet. "I will say this one time and one time only, so listen up. No one gets to be a hero, here. No one gets to leave until we are done. If you all play nicely, every last one of you will walk out of here with your lives. Got it?"

When no one answered, the man shook his head. "See? Now, this is a bad start. Two rules: when I talk, you listen. When I *tell you* to talk, you talk. Let's try this again." He made a show of exaggerating what he said next. "If you all play nicely, every last one of you will walk out of here with your lives. Got it?"

"Got it," the fourteen hostages said in robotic unison.

"Good. First things first, though."

Gun still raised, the man herded the scattered phones together with his foot until a haphazard pile rested at his shoes. Like a soccer player dribbling a ball between his feet, the man worked the phone pile to the south wall, where no hostages were within ten feet. He pointed at the pile with the gun.

"This wall is off limits. Anyone goes near the phones or the wall and they'll find a bullet in their belly. Got it?"

Sara watched the man's face as he spoke, once again overcome by the feeling that she'd met him before. The way he spoke—the *way* he formed his words—the cutting mockery in his tone, the sharp criticism under the thin lacquer of civility, the way he had seemed, and still *did* seem, incapable of taking an entire room hostage at gunpoint. His whole being screamed deception, and yet...

Sara glanced at Janice. The big woman was slumped on her left side, her hand still over her chest. Janice's eyes were focused on the ceiling, her lips pursed as she tried to steady her breathing. Sara knew that if Janice didn't get medical attention immediately, she'd die in the very diner she daily vowed to walk away from.

The man walked to the middle of the diner and swept the gun around the room.

"You are all here for a reason. Your lives have pointed you, have *steered* you, to this very diner at this precise time."

Janice let out a long moan and slumped all the way to the floor. Her right hand clawed at her chest, her breath now staccato gasps.

"Pl-please … l-let me …" another agonized moan cut off her words.

Sara felt utterly helpless. If she made a move toward Janice, they'd both be shot. There was nothing she could do for her. There was nothing anyone could do for her. The realization ripped her apart. Even though Janice wasn't the most pleasant person in Lewiston, Sara considered her a friend. And friends didn't let friends die without trying to intervene. But there was nothing she could do. She knew it, and she hoped Janice knew it, too.

The man with the gun looked at Janice, cocked his head to the side like a curious puppy. But his eyes weren't that of a domestic animal. His eyes were wild, sinister. He walked over to Janice, stooped down beside her. Reaching out with his free hand, he touched her shoulder with his long fingers. At his touch, Janice shrieked. Her body trembled with pain and terror as the man stroked first her shoulder and then her cheek. He turned from her to address the diner hostages, the backs of his first two fingers never leaving Janice's cheek.

"You are all here to find life in the face of death. Your freedom is a choice. *You* get to decide whether you walk out of here. *You* get to choose between life and death. Whatever happens over the course of the next few moments is *yours* to choose. All you have to do is let out that one thing you keep locked away in the abysmal dungeon of your soul. Set it free, and *you* will be free. It is *your* choice. I cannot make it for you. I can only implore you to make the *right* choice. Liberation breeds liberation. Freedom begets freedom. The choice is yours and yours alone."

Sara's head swam with the man's words.

What is he talking about? He's obviously crazy. Probably a lunatic who forgot to take his meds this morning.

And yet she felt her heart responding to his confusing message, felt the hope his words offered. Freedom. A chance to walk out of the diner with her life. The opportunity to finish college, maybe even to meet someone and to start a family. Freedom. Liberation. The man had said the choice was hers. All she had to do was make it. But were his words nothing more than babble from a mentally unstable soul? Or were they legitimate enough to take seriously?

The man turned back to Janice, continued to stroke her cheek with the backs of his long fingers.

"Unfortunately, some of us will never get the opportunity to choose freedom. Outside the diner door, there are thousands of walking dead men and women. They'll never get the chance I'm offering you. They'll never get the opportunity to open their soul's prison door and allow what is inside to roam free. They will die without understanding true freedom." The man ran his hand gently through Janice's hair.

"Like poor Janice, here. She'll never get to know liberation. She'll never get to face the prisoner of her soul—the secret menace that keeps her from freedom. She is dying even as I speak and will never have a chance to let her beast out. It's tragic, really."

Janice moaned and tears streamed down her cheeks.

The man wiped a tear from Janice's cheek. "Should I tell them, Janice? Should I unleash your prisoner?"

Janice shook her head, shrieked in pain as the tears continued to flow.

"Should I tell them you've been stealing money for years from this very diner? *Fourteen* years, to be exact? Should I tell them you've been giving the money to your worthless husband to fuel his drug habit so he doesn't beat you senseless? What is it now, Janice? Meth? Is he cooking meth now? Pills, heroin, meth, whatever it is, *you* have been feeding it. *You* have been the enabler, Janice, because you feel like you are too fat to love. You feed his addiction while you feed your face. You do it because you feel inferior and you crave his fake acceptance as you crave cheeseburgers."

Janice's breath was dangerously short, and her body trembled as she clawed at her chest.

"If only you could've told them, Janice. If only you could've let your demons out."

Sara watched in horror as the man raised the gun from his side. He stood up, took two steps back.

"But you won't get that opportunity, will you, Janice?

You'll die enslaved." His lips parted into an insidious, toothy smile. "Sorry, Janice."

The man pulled the trigger and the shot boomed in the small diner. Janice's head exploded before Sara had time to look away. She felt her stomach lurch, felt the bile climb to the back of her throat. She couldn't look, wouldn't look. A woman sitting at one of the booths was crying, others were trying to compose themselves for fear they were next. Sara put her head down and refused to look up. A solitary sob bubbled into her chest, and she clenched every muscle in her body to ward it off.

I'm never getting out of here! I'm going to die here!

She heard the man's footsteps as he walked back to the center of the room.

"Bill and Carl. Take the body into the kitchen. And don't try anything." A pause. "Do it now!"

Sara heard Bill and Carl—whoever they were—quickly move to Janice's body. After some grunting and whispers back and forth, the two men decided to drag Janice's body instead of trying to pick it up. She was a big woman, and Sara understood their decision, but the wet sound of the body being dragged across the tile floor was almost too much. After a few moments of awful silence, she heard the men's footsteps as they came back into the diner.

"Well done, gentlemen," the man with the gun said. Only then did Sara look up. When she saw the dark crimson smear of blood on the tiles, she nearly retched. She tried not to notice the bloody, gray blobs that stuck to the wall and suctioned to the floor, but she couldn't help but think Janice's brains belonged inside her head and not on the cold, unforgiving tiles of the diner she said she hated but secretly loved.

And there was something else.

How had the man known all that about Janice? How had he even known her name*? And Bill's and Carl's? Could he have been making up all the stuff about the money and the*

9

drugs?

But somehow Sara knew the man wasn't lying. Somehow she knew everything he had said had been spot-on. She knew it as she knew she'd seen him somewhere before. She knew it as she knew she'd *talked* to him in some other time and in some other place.

"And then there were thirteen," the man said. He pulled a table to the center of the room and pointed at the waitress station with the gun. "Okay. Everyone move by Sara, please. I'm getting tired of standing. I'm only going to say it once, so please just do it quickly."

As one, thirteen bodies made their way across the diner's tiled floor. A woman settled at her left, and Carl took the place on her right. For the first time, Sara truly assessed the diner hostages. Eight of the hostages were men, none of them as young as Sara's twenty years. If Sara had to guess, four were in their fifties and sixties, one was in his seventies, and two were in their early forties. Only one looked younger than thirty-five, and he took his place on the floor two men to her right. He sat Indian-style, his elbows on his thighs, slightly further out from the other two men, as the makeshift line of bodies curved ever-so-slightly. In any other situation, Sara might have considered him attractive, with his slightly mussed acorn-brown hair and short, smidgen-darker cheek stubble. When he glanced her way, she saw he had milk-chocolate eyes that were thoughtful and alive. Hope rose in her chest. Maybe this man would be the one to save them all. He was the youngest, and his slender frame didn't advertise anything but hard, lean muscle underneath his grey hoodie. Sara quickly dismissed the thought. It was unfair to place her hope in anyone else. A gun made everyone equal.

Just keep your head down and don't draw attention to yourself.

The other five hostages were women, three of them the

wives of the sixty-something husbands, and two of them thirty-somethings who had been enjoying their Saturday morning lattes before the chaos started. But it had turned the page from chaos, hadn't it? Wasn't the next page all about carnage? Weren't thirteen people sitting like elementary students on a reading rug while a *murderer* with a gun spoke nonsense about demons in their souls and freedom from the beasts within? Hadn't he just *killed Janice*?

The man smiled, placed his right hand holding the gun atop his thigh and kept it aimed at the group.

"Now, this is better. More comfortable. So, who wants to go first?"

Silence.

"I asked who wants to go first?"

Sara felt her heartbeat accelerate even more than it already had.

What is he talking about?! What are we supposed to volunteer for?!

Perhaps it was because he had been selected by the man with the gun to carry Janice's body to the kitchen, or perhaps it was because he had much more courage than Sara. Whatever the case, Carl ventured the question everyone was thinking.

"Uh—what do you—what are we supposed to ..."

The man's smile faded. His feral eyes showed fire.

"I thought I went over this, Carl. And now you're sitting here sputtering like an idiot. It's all about freedom. Freedom from the thing inside you no one knows about. The deepest, darkest thing that you have never told a soul about. I guess you can call this a confession, of sorts. But with confession comes freedom."

"Who—who are you? How do you know my name?" Carl was much braver than Sara would ever be.

The man cocked his head to the side again the same way he had before he'd shot Janice. Sara felt a chill dance on her spine.

"Who am I? Who am *I*? It really doesn't matter who I am. What matters is what I *know*. But because you asked for a name, I'll give you one suitable for our circumstance. You may call me the Accuser. I am, in essence, accusing you all of harboring a beast within. I am here to remind you that by recognizing and taking ownership of that which lives inside you, you can be free."

"But, how did you know my …"

The man—the *Accuser*—held up his left hand. "Carl, Carl, Carl. You didn't hear what I just said. The fact that I know your name should be the least of your concerns. The fact that I know much more should have you squirming where you sit. How are you enjoying your retirement, by the way?"

Sara chanced a glance at Carl, saw the squat, bald man was flummoxed by the question.

"It was a simple question, Carl. Your retirement from the bank. Are you enjoying it?"

"What are you …"

The man sighed. "Maybe I need to explain a little more about what is happening here. I will only do this once, so make sure you pay attention. I am accusing you of your most secret infraction. I am probing your soul, drilling into your being to help you expose your beast to the world. You will either unleash your beast, or you will die. It is that simple. I have come to give you freedom. There is no need to hide behind your shame once it is exposed to the world. This is where true liberation begins."

The man looked each hostage in the eye, and Sara once again felt a twinge of familiarity and, strangely, a twinge of guilt.

"I am going to give you a choice. You will bare your soul to the room, or you will die. It is simple, really. As the Accuser, it is my duty to find fault in you. It is also my duty to destroy

12

you, should you choose against liberation. Each of you will get a turn. Have I made myself clear?"

Carl cleared his throat. "Uh—what—how will you know …"

"It is not for you to know *how* I know, Carl. It is better for you to *know* that I know. You need to understand that your sins will be revealed to the room no matter what you choose. The only difference is that in one scenario you will have a bullet in your belly. It is your choice. *You* get to choose. The reality is that you are all pathetic, wretched creatures not worthy to suck in the oxygen you breathe. You are all vile, you are all worthless. You are all chiefs of sinners. I am accusing you all of being lower than dirt and more rancid than excrement. Now you get to choose freedom or death. Do you understand, Carl?"

Sara glanced at Carl again. The man's forehead glistened with sweat.

"Y—yes. I think I understand."

The man smiled, his once seawater blue eyes beginning to smolder with blackness. "Good. You get to go first. When I ask you this question, you have thirty seconds to begin your response. I urge you to be honest. You have no idea what I know. Are you ready, Carl?"

Sara's heart pounded.

This man is crazy. We are all going to die, today!

"I-I'm ready," Carl said, his voice catching for a moment.

The man's lips peeled back to reveal his most evil smile yet.

"Carl Berryman, I accuse you of harboring a secret infraction. You may choose freedom, or you may choose death. What is your greatest sin?"

Chapter Two

ARL TOOK A DEEP BREATH, LET IT OUT. SARA COULD see the man trembling in her peripherals. A terrible silence broken only by Carl's staccato breaths, filled the diner.

Say something!

Carl cleared his throat. "Uh—I—I guess I ..."

The Accuser's eyes narrowed in mockery. "You *guess*, Carl? You *guess*? Is this how you justify your life's most revolting stain? You *guess*?" He walked closer, extended his arm to full length, pointed the gun directly at Carl's forehead. "You're going to have to do better than that, you pathetic worm. Tell them. *Tell* them."

Sara felt something wet and warm soak into her jeans and spread over the side of her leg. She instinctively looked at the floor and felt her stomach turn at the sight of the yellowish pool that puddled beneath Carl and spread to her thigh. In any other situation she might have retched. She understood why Carl's bladder had released. It could just as easily have been hers.

"Okay, okay," Carl said. "I'll tell you. But—please ..."

"You're wasting my time, Carl," the Accuser said. "Now. Start speaking."

Carl took another deep breath, let it out with a half-sob. He quickly sucked in his emotion, a strange sound that was a mixture of a moan and a hiccup.

"My—my greatest sin," Carl said. "I was—I was in college,

and—and I broke into the registrar's office."

The Accuser's face turned to stone. His now black eyes smoldered, the muscles of his jaw clenched and unclenched ferociously as Carl continued.

"I was failing accounting—I needed at least a C to get into grad school. I didn't know how I was going to …"

Sara felt the warm blood spatter on her cheek before she realized the Accuser had pulled the trigger. Her eardrums felt as if they were pulsing, the room spun and she thought she'd pass out. She could barely hear the shocked screams of the other hostages, but she heard clear as a bullhorn the Accuser's voice.

"Liar! You *lied*, Carl! Your greatest sin, the one you've never told a soul, is that you are cheating on your wife with a bank teller! You lied, and you *died!*" He wiped the corner of his mouth where a fleck of spittle had settled in his scruff. "Two people, drag his worthless carcass into the kitchen! *Now!*"

Sara felt anchored to the floor. She knew she should do as the Accuser had commanded, knew her life depended on heeding his instruction, but the enormity of the situation paralyzed her. Where were the police? Shouldn't they be bursting through the door at any moment? Shouldn't they have heard the gunshots that had extinguished lives before her eyes? But the icy bucket of cruel reality swept over her. It was the cruel reality that cared nothing for her nor any of the hostages in the diner. The police wouldn't be coming. Not today. The Accuser had been smart in picking this morning to play his demented game. The Lewiston Community Days were taking place in Homeyer Park five miles west of Main Street where Ned's Diner was located. The entire force of barely-apt lawmen would be moseying around the crowd of townsfolk who were no doubt already gathering to set their children loose on the inflatable games so they could gorge themselves on chili and artery-clogging carnival food. This was the reality Sara found herself in. No one was coming to help. Not today. Not ever. And there was the horrific reality that she was sitting next to a man whose head had been blown open, his blood and brain bits splattered on her clothes and skin. She felt her stomach lurch, and this time she couldn't keep its contents from bursting forth. Quickly spinning, she vomited her thankfully light breakfast of yogurt and wheat toast onto the tiles. She wiped her mouth with the back of her wrist and vowed she wouldn't look at Carl's body as she heard it being carried to the kitchen.

Don't look, don't look, don't look!

Sara turned back around, her eyes clenched shut against the gruesome scene. She heard footsteps returning from the kitchen, heard two bodies—both to the right of her—settle onto the floor with the other hostages. The Accuser's voice boomed into the diner.

"Carl was foolish. He didn't realize I knew about his infidelity. He thought he could conceal his sin, keep it locked in the dungeon of his soul forever. But I am the exposer. I'm the *accuser*. Nothing is hidden from me. *Nothing*. Though your sin be as black as night, my accusations will make you white as snow. Through shame, you will know freedom. I am *freeing* you, don't you get it? Once you make the decision to release your sin to the world, you can forget about it. Will you be seen differently in the eyes of the world? Perhaps. But you will be able to live in complete and absolute freedom from the thing that once held you captive because *you have a chance to make it your own.* In essence, your *sin* is what will free you. The evil you perceive about yourself is actually a *good thing.* But first it has to be worked to the surface like a splinter under the skin. Before freedom, there must be pain."

When the Accuser stopped speaking, Sara finally opened her eyes. The first thing she saw was her blood-spattered jeans and the black smears of blood near her right thigh where Carl's body had been dragged over the tiles.

"Who wants to go next?" the Accuser asked, his gun dancing over his hostages. "Who wants to find freedom?"

Sara's heart cannoned.

Not me! Please, God—not me!

The Accuser nodded. "Fine. I'll pick. Abigail Morris, you are up."

Sara let out her breath through her teeth. It wasn't her. She didn't have to risk a bullet hole through the forehead—yet.

But, someone else does…

"Why don't you stand up, Abigail. Come stand by me so everyone can see you." The Accuser motioned with his gun, and Abigail, a sixty-something, skinny woman with reddish-brown hair stood from the group. Sara's heart went out to her, but there was nothing she could do. She glanced briefly at the young man she hoped would rescue them, saw his eyes squinted in either deep thought or intense focus. She hoped his fixed concentration meant he was formulating a plan for how to get the hostages to safety. But that was only hope. As Abigail stepped next to the Accuser, her green eyes spilling over with tears, her body as fragile as a baby bird's, Sara knew they wouldn't all make it out of the diner alive. Maybe *none* of them would make it out alive.

The Accuser smiled and draped his left arm around Abigail's shoulders. She shrieked in response. He laughed.

"There's no need to fear freedom, Abigail. If you are honest in your admission, you will walk out the front door a brand new woman. How does that sound?"

Abigail whimpered in response.

"Let's begin." The Accuser removed his arm from Abigail's shoulders and took a step back. He fixed the gun on her forehead.

"Abigail Morris. I accuse you of a vile sin. You are worthless and beyond love as you harbor your secret inside of you. You are wretched beyond words as your sin festers like a boil on your soul. Tell them, Abigail. It is for freedom that I've come. *Your* freedom. Tell them your deepest, darkest sin."

Chapter Three

ABIGAIL MORRIS COULDN'T COM-
pose herself enough to speak. Tears and snot
mingled on her upper lip and chin, and the air she sucked
in was cut by sobs. Sara pleaded with the woman, begged
her, willed her with her mind to *say* something, to say
anything. She knew the Accuser wouldn't wait forever.
He'd already discharged his weapon twice, and with star-
tling swiftness. Abigail's life depended upon whether she
could compose herself enough to play his sadistic game.

But she has to play the game the right way...

"I—I've never told anyone this," Abigail started.
"It—it's not something I'm proud of."

"Why not just cut to the chase, Abigail. Your blub-
bering and sniveling is pathetic. *You* are the sinner. It
was *you* who made the choice so many years ago. You
will receive no sympathy from us, worthless woman. *You*
have perpetuated your own shame."

The Accuser pressed the barrel of his gun to Abigail's
temple. "Speak, woman."

Abigail swiped her nose with the back of her hand and
tried her best to compose herself.

"Okay! Okay! I—I watched my mother die! She
drowned! I couldn't jump in and save her!"

The Accuser's lips raised into a demonic smile. "You *couldn't* or you, *didn't*, Abigail? Which one is it? You were *helpless* to save your mother, or you *could have* tried harder to get her out of that lake?"

Abigail shook like a leaf. "No—stop! I couldn't--"

"You allowed your mother to drown!" the Accuser's voice rose in volume with each word. "You could have saved her life! You could have pulled her out of the driver's seat, and you know it! Instead, you chose to swim to the surface yourself!"

"No! I—it was dark and I was—I was only seven!"

"Excuses! Your whole life has been excuses! So much therapy, so much *whining!*"

Abigail sobbed so hard she started to cough. The Accuser seemed to delight in watching her suffer. Sara wished she could intervene, wished she could make it stop. But she knew if she moved, her head would be blown from her shoulders.

"You are nothing but excuses, Abigail! Your marriage failed, but it wasn't *your fault*, was it? Your kids don't speak to you anymore, but it is *their problem*, right? You are *never* the cause of the conflict, are you?"

"Please—stop!"

"You're a disease, Abigail! You infect the world with your self-pity! You make us all sick with your *lies*! The fact is, you've never forgiven yourself for *killing your mother!*"

"I—I didn't kill her! She swerved to miss a deer and …"

The Accuser laughed, his voice dripping with mockery. "You didn't make her swerve off the road, but you killed her when you decided your life was more important than hers. When your mother's car broke through the guardrail and rolled into the lake, you never thought twice

19

about swimming to the surface."

"It was so dark …"

"It wasn't dark enough for you to swim to the surface! You killed her, Abigail! It is *your fault* your mother is dead! It is *your fault* she never had the opportunity to conceive another child! It is *your fault* your father turned into an alcoholic, and it is *your fault* he beat you when he was drunk!"

"God—please!"

The Accuser snatched a handful of her hair and pulled her head back.

"There is no God, right? Isn't that what you've been telling people for years? And now you have the gall to call out to Him?"

"P—please, sir—I …"

The Accuser brought his face to Abigail's cheek. He placed his lips to her ear and viciously whispered loud enough for the other hostages to hear:

"There is no god who can save you, Abigail. *I'm* the only god, today, and my purpose is to refine you by fire so that you might save yourself."

Abigail trembled.

"Say it, Abigail," the Accuser whispered. "Tell them you killed your mother."

"I—I killed my mother."

The Accuser yanked her hair, and Sara thought for sure a handful would be ripped from Abigail's scalp.

"Louder, Abigail. Tell them you're a murderer. Tell them you killed your mother."

"I killed my mother."

"Louder!" the Accuser boomed.

"I killed my mother!" Abigail shrieked. The Accuser let go of her hair and shoved her to the floor. She crumpled like a ragdoll, a heaving, sobbing mess.

"Was that so hard, Abigail? You are a murderer, a liar and a horrible excuse for a human being. You don't deserve to live and breathe."

Abigail continued to sob. Sara knew the woman was in another place, now. She wasn't on the floor of Ned's Diner. She was back at the lake, back at the scene of her supposed crime.

"It's too much, isn't it Abigail?" The Accuser's voice softened to a sickening faux compassion.

Abigail only sobbed in response.

"You've thought about ending your life many times. When your father beat you. When your husband left you. When your kids stopped calling." The Accuser stooped over Abigail's crumpled being.

"You know you wanted to die—*want* to die. There's no reason for you to live, no purpose for you to pursue. You're a hollow shell of a human. You *know* I'm right, Abigail."

Sara watched in horror as the Accuser flipped the gun in his hand so he held the barrel. The handle was extended to Abigail.

"You know you want to end it, Abigail. Death is a form of freedom. It is a release from the burdens you created for yourself. I'm offering you freedom right now. Look up, Abigail."

Abigail obeyed, and Sara's stomach roiled.

What is he doing?

"Take the gun, Abigail. Find freedom."

Abigail looked at the gun and then at the Accuser.

"Wh—what are you asking me to …"

"I'm not asking you to do anything you haven't thought of yourself. I'm offering you the best kind of freedom. It is a permanent release from the pain you've rained upon your life for so many years. It is the release from failure

21

and the oppression of living as a murderer. You know you want to, Abigail. In your death you will find freedom. Take the gun."

Sara could hardly breathe as Abigail swiped the snot and tears from her face and seemed to consider the proffered gun in a way that made Sara want to cry out.

"Freedom is yours, Abigail. Take the gun. Do it."

Sara was horrified that she *wanted* Abigail to take the gun. But it wasn't for the same reason the Accuser wanted her to take it. The gun could mean freedom—*literal* freedom. And if Abigail realized she actually had another option if she chose to take the gun, all the hostages would find such freedom.

Take the gun! Turn it on him!

But as Sara watched Abigail consider the gun, Sara knew she wouldn't be walking out of the diner as a free woman.

"Take it, Abigail," the Accuser whispered. "Go on. Take it."

Abigail took a deep breath, let it out. Her eyes conveyed a strange longing for what the gun could offer. Sara saw it all in Abigail's eyes. The woman was weary, tired and worn. She'd been buffeted by life and lived under the self-imposed sentence of a murderer. The Accuser was only offering her something she'd probably considered numerous times in her life. And the Accuser knew Abigail as he had known Carl. He *knew* her history, knew her greatest shortcomings, knew her absolute and horrible guilt.

She's going to take the gun. She's going to use it on herself...

Abigail slowly reached for the gun. As she did, the sobbing started again. It was a sobbing of finality, of resolution. She'd made up her mind and there was no turning back.

"That's good, Abigail. That's good," the Accuser said.

Abigail's hand was on the gun, and the Accuser took a step backward.

"You're making the right decision, Abigail. Death is permanent freedom. No more pain, no more shame. You no longer will have to live with the fact that you are a murderer posing as a free woman."

Abigail wrapped her hand around the handle, and the Accuser completely let go of the barrel. He took another step back as Abigail raised herself to her feet.

"Now, turn the gun and put it to your temple. It's quick and painless freedom, Abigail. Much less pain than the time you sliced your wrists."

Someone needs to stop her! Someone needs to do something!

Abigail pressed the gun against her forehead, her eyes glazed with tears.

"Just pull the trigger, Abigail. Free yourself from the misery you created. Pull the trigger. Gain liberation."

Abigail trembled and her breathing came faster. Sara felt as if all the air had been sucked out of the diner.

"Do it, Abigail!" the Accuser boomed.

Abigail pulled the trigger.

Chapter Four

WHEN SARA OPENED HER EYES again, Abigail's body had been carried to the kitchen. Sara's ears rung, and new blood speckled her jeans. The horror of what had transpired felt far away, as if it hadn't occurred in real-time right in front of her, but in some foreign land. As on the evening news, horrible things always happened, but those horrible things weren't ever in the here and now.

Until they were.

The Accuser had taken his gun back and now sat on the tabletop, and surveying the twelve remaining hostages. He had escaped the blood spatter from Abigail's shot, but Sara saw the evidence that she had, indeed, pulled the trigger. Sara couldn't hide from the fact that such an atrocity hadn't happened in a distant land, but in Lewiston, Ohio, in the middle of Ned's Diner.

"Abigail made a wise choice," the Accuser said. "She gave in to the urge to end her struggles. She was a murderer, a liar, a whiner. She has finally found rest in death."

Sara glanced at the young man. His brown eyes studied the floor, his face expressionless.

We need to do something...

"You all are as guilty as Abigail," the Accuser continued.

"You all are as sick, as diseased."

Sara fought back the shiver that ran down her spine. The sense that she had met the Accuser before, that she knew his voice, his biting criticism, came back to her again.

Who is he?

"Who will be next?" the Accuser asked.

"Why would any of us volunteer?" a male voice asked. "The first two who played your sick game died!"

Sara was shocked. Who had had the nerve to speak to the Accuser like that?

The Accuser smiled. "Bill, Bill, Bill. I'm so glad you volunteered."

Sara didn't have a clear view of Bill, but he sat on her left a few people down from her.

"I didn't volunteer," Bill answered. "I'm not playing your game."

The Accuser's smile never wavered. "That's where you're wrong, Bill. You *will* play the game. You have no choice."

"But you said we all had choices," Bill said quickly. "You said we get to make the choice whether we live or die. I choose life."

"Obviously you didn't listen, Bill," the Accuser said, scooting off the tabletop. His eyes flickered in anger, but his feral smile never left his lips.

"You are correct when you say you have a choice. But your choice only comes after I accuse you of the most heinous sin you've ever committed. You have two options: freedom or death."

"You're talking in circles," Bill said. "You speak of freedom and death, but Abigail killed herself and you called it freedom. It seems to me you can't have it both ways."

"Abigail found freedom in her sin. She chose a different kind of freedom than you might choose, Bill, but she found freedom."

"You're insane!"

The Accuser's smile vanished. His stubbled face was stone, his eyes ablaze.

"I am the most lucid person in the room. I see your sin, and I am offering you a chance to own it. In that ownership, you will find freedom."

Bill laughed. "So you get to make all the rules? You get to determine whether we live or die? Who gave you that authority?"

The Accuser's sinister smile returned. "No one gave me authority. I am my own authority. I set up dominion here. This diner is *mine* now."

Bill laughed again. "This is ludicrous! You are completely ins–"

The shot rang out before Sara had time to prepare herself for it. When her brain finally registered what had happened, she clenched her eyes shut again.

No—no!

"Get his body into the kitchen!" the Accuser said. "Now!"

***

"Who is next?" the Accuser asked a few minutes after Bill's body had successfully been carried to the kitchen.

This is how we all will die. One by one. Is this game even able to be won?

"How about you, Brian? Why don't you stand and join me here."

Sara heard the pop of tired knees as Brian stood from the group. When she saw he was the oldest man in the diner, her heart sank. Not only did Brian have no chance of survival himself, but he had no chance to save the rest of them from certain death. The man was old in every sense of the word. His thin frame and age-spotted face set him apart from the rest of the hostages. His hair was a tangle of white spider web strands, and he wore khaki pants and a tucked-in baby blue button down.

"Brian Dennison. You are the eldest of our band of sinners," the Accuser said, clapping the old man on the back. Brian's face was expressionless.

"You're a veteran of the Second World War," the Accuser continued. "You are respected wherever you go. But I know the truth, Brian. You are honored in the eyes of men, but your honor is blackened by sin. What if they knew the truth? What if they were aware of your hypocrisy? What if they really *knew* you?"

The old man's blue eyes never left the wall behind the waitress station. When he spoke, his voice was measured, even.

"I'm old. I've lived my life. I've stared Nazi soldiers in the face, and I've been a prisoner of war. I've had a gun pointed at me many times, son, and I'm not afraid of you or any bullet that gun can fire."

The Accuser laughed. "Your courage is impressive, albeit misguided. You are correct to say you shouldn't fear me, and I know you don't. You truly believe your sin was so far in the past that the statute of limitations has run out on it. You think that just because you committed a horrific act decades ago, time has erased your iniquity."

"I know I have paid for whatever sins I have committed," Brian answered. "I have been a good man. Not a perfect man, but a good one. I can live with myself. I can look at myself in the mirror every day."

The Accuser laughed again, twirled the gun in his hand.

"You can look at yourself in the mirror because you've justified your sin. You've told yourself that you would never commit the act you did outside the confines of war. Isn't that so?"

"I don't have to answer to you, son."

The Accuser jammed the gun against the old man's temple.

"You have to answer to yourself. You have been suppressing your horrific sin for decades, and now you are going to face it."

"My conscience is clean."

"Is it?"

"Yes."

The Accuser narrowed his eyes. "Brian Dennison, I accuse you of committing a terrible sin. You may choose freedom or death. The decision is yours. Speak."

***

SARA watched as the old man stood stoically, heroically to the Accuser's left. Silence filled the diner as the eleven remaining hostages and the Accuser waited for Brian Dennison to speak.

This isn't going to end well. He is going to end up dead like the rest of them...

"I have nothing to say. I am ready to die, if you are ready to kill me." The old man clenched his jaw once, but his eyes never left the wall.

"You would really choose death over freedom?" the Accuser asked. "You would choose to be buried in your filth?"

"I choose to die with honor."

The Accuser's evil smile returned. "Always the soldier."

Sara's heart pounded as she watched the scene unfold. The Accuser walked a full circle around the old man.

"What if I told them, Brian? You haven't told a soul. You didn't even tell your wife, may she rest in peace. What you did violated the ethics of humanity, do you realize that?"

A solitary tear trickled from the old man's right eye. The Accuser's smile widened.

"You do realize it, don't you? You sinned against your code

of honor, the *world's* code of honor. And, why? Because you were *there*? Because she was *there*? Because you thought your sin couldn't jump an ocean? Because you thought you had buried it in France all those years ago?"

More tears fell from the old man's eyes. He clenched his jaw and his Adam's apple bobbed up and down as he tried to keep his emotions at bay.

The Accuser kept at it, his eyes ablaze, his sinister smile fueled by the old man's tears.

"And now you stand here silent. Your perceived honor is intact. But I ask you, Brian, is it really honor if you stand silent against your atrocity? Aren't you, in effect, lying by omission?"

The old man's chin began to tremble and his tears fell steadily.

"And what of that poor girl?" the Accuser continued. "You didn't even know her name, did you? You don't *want* to know her name."

Sara could only watch in speechless horror as Brian Dennison, veteran of the Second World War, cracked.

"I didn't mean ..."

The Accuser pounced at the opening. "What didn't you mean, Brian? You didn't mean to violate a poor, defenseless girl? You didn't mean to violate *Dominique*?"

The old man sucked in a breath when the Accuser said the girl's name. His chin trembled faster, his voice came out broken and weary.

"No—please—don't say ..."

"Don't say what, Brian? The poor girl's name? Dominique? Dominique? *Dominique*?"

"I never—I wish I could ..."

"I wish you could have been straight with us, Brian," the Accuser said, thrusting the gun into the old man's temple. "I wish you would've seen the benefit in telling them the story yourself."

All Brian Dennison could do was cry.

The Accuser cocked his head. "You know what, Brian? I'm feeling generous today. I might have opened the lid on your sin, but there's still more inside the can. Are you willing to dump the can, Brian? Are you willing to tell them the entire story yourself? If you tell them, you will live. If you decide to blubber here like a scolded child, you'll die. The choice is yours."

Tell us! Tell us so you can live—so that we *can live!*

The old man took a deep breath, swiped his cheeks with the back of his age-spotted hand.

"Okay. Okay. I'll tell you all the story. But you have to remember, it was many years ago."

"They need not hear a justification for your sin, Brian. All they need is the story," the Accuser said. "You have thirty seconds to start."

Sara saw a flash out of the corner of her eye. Someone—one of the men in his sixties—had sprung from his seat. He hurled his body at the Accuser, who still had his gun at Brian Dennison's temple. Startled only for a moment, the Accuser flicked the gun at the approaching man and squeezed the trigger twice. The man was short, bald and paunchy-stomached, no match for the lightening-quick Accuser. The former clutched his gut and fell to the tile floor with a surprised moan. A pool of blood formed immediately where he fell and the Accuser pointed the gun at his head for a kill shot.

"Bad move, Ron."

Brian Dennison's tired fist shot from his side and clipped the Accuser's cheek. It was a heroic punch, but not enough to keep the Accuser from pulling the trigger to finish off Ron. Sara watched in stunned horror as the Accuser pivoted and fired two shots at the old man. Both shots hit Brian Dennison in the chest, and the old man stumbled backward twice before falling over a table.

"I expected more from you, Brian," the Accuser said, his shoes crunching over broken glass as he crossed to where Brian Dennison lay gasping for breath.

"I thought you were coming to your senses. And then you go and do something stupid to get yourself killed. What would Dominique say about that, hmm? Do you think she'd be happy to know you're dying in the United States in a pool of your own blood? I think she'd be happy to hear it. I *know* she'd be happy to hear it. That September day in 1943, you *destroyed her life*. There's no honor in destruction, Brian. None at all."

Brian Dennison heaved and coughed. "I've made my peace with God. Only He is fit to judge …"

The Accuser's gun boomed again and silenced Brian Dennison forever.

"God is dead, Brian," the Accuser said as he looked down on the old man's body. "He is dead here on this planet of sin and degradation. Vermin like you are supposed to be a reflection of His glory. Instead, you justify your abominable actions in the name of His grace, and you pervert His statutes by molding them to shape your own worldview. He is dead. You killed Him, or at least the idea of Him. Why would anyone want to serve a rapist's God?"

Sara felt numb to everything. More people had been shot right in front of her, more lives had been extinguished by a madman playing a childish game. She was appalled by how quickly death became the norm, how her own self-preservation trumped anything else. What was she, if not a selfish monster that only cared for her own safety and breathed a sigh of relief every time the Accuser pulled the trigger and a bullet didn't puncture her skin. She was alive and others were dead. She still had a pinprick's chance at freedom, while those the Accuser had killed had none. Maybe the Accuser was correct in his assessment. Maybe she was vermin; maybe they *all* were vermin. She knew beyond the shadow of a doubt she'd heard his voice before, and she knew beyond the shadow of a doubt that he was *right* about some things.

And that realization should have terrified her. Instead, it felt like acceptance.

It felt like nothing.

Chapter Five

AFTER BOTH BODIES HAD BEEN taken to the kitchen, the Accuser sat on his table-top and surveyed the remaining hostages in silence.

"This hasn't been going well for you, I'm afraid. I've given you the option of freedom and none of the dead opted to experience liberation. Why is that? Do you fear freedom? Do you fear that which you've never experienced? Do you fear that which you can't possibly understand in your lowly states?"

Sara glanced at the young man. He was watching the Accuser's every move, studying the Accuser as one pours over vital information. Sara wasn't the only one to take notice. The Accuser leaned forward, looked directly at the young man. For a moment—and for just a moment—Sara saw a flicker of something new in the Accuser eyes. What was it?

Fear...

"I don't recognize you," the Accuser said, nodding at the young man. His voice was even, steady. It betrayed nothing except a lack of the bravado that had been so pronounced every other time he had spoken.

The young man said nothing, only continued to study the Accuser with his deep chocolate eyes.

The Accuser smiled, but the smile was forced and uncomfortable. There was definitely something different about the

Accuser's demeanor, Sara was sure of it.

"I said I don't recognize you. And I recognize everyone."

The young man breathed in through his nose, exhaled.

"I recognize you."

The Accuser's smile dropped. His eyes squinted into vicious, razor-blade slits.

What is going on?

"What does that mean? Are you mocking me?"

The young man tilted his head slightly. His voice was as peaceful as a placid lake.

"I'm not mocking you. I'm simply saying I recognize you."

The Accuser was visibly taken aback. Sara wondered what the young man meant. Did he, too, recognize the Accuser's voice and deriding tone? Did he, too, know him from somewhere?

"Why is it I don't know you?" the Accuser said, more to himself than to the young man. "I know the sins of humanity. I've accused in China and India, in Canada and Kenya. Yet, I don't recognize your sins." The Accuser chuckled uncomfortably. "You are human, aren't you?"

"I am."

"And yet I don't know your greatest iniquity."

The young man didn't answer, only continued to study the Accuser. The Accuser held the young man's gaze for a moment before looking away. Sara couldn't believe it. The Accuser was unnerved. But why?

"It is time we continue. Who will go next?"

Sara's eyes immediately went to the tile floor. Perhaps not looking at the Accuser would keep him from accusing her.

"Sara Thompson. Please come stand beside me."

Please, God—no!

Sara's stomach dropped and her bladder threatened to release. A buzzing sound filled her ears, and her chest felt as if it had been slugged by a tire iron.

This is it—this is how I will die!

"Sara. Come here. Now. I won't ask again."

Sara willed her legs to move. They felt weightless beneath her, and she stumbled the first time she tried to stand.

Get up! Get up! Get up!

Knowing time wasn't on her side, Sara finally managed to get to her feet. For a terrible moment, the room spun, and she thought she'd pass out.

"Sara, Sara, Sara. So good to see you again." As he had with the others, the Accuser put his arm around her shoulders. His touch repulsed and terrified her at the same time.

Please—no! Don't do this!

The young man was looking at her, his brown eyes seeming to search her the way he had the Accuser. The effect his gaze had on her was strange, considering the circumstances. His eyes conveyed peace, tranquility and—yes—*hope*.

"Sara, I implore you to search your heart and soul in these next few moments," the Accuser said, knocking her back to reality. He was close to her—too close. His eyes were alive and full of malice, his breath hot and sulfuric on her cheek. He looked at her with the assuredness that it was his *right* to accuse her, his *right* to annihilate her with his venomous words. Sara knew just by his look that he wasn't used to being challenged, and somewhere behind the feral quality of his eyes, a tension brewed. The young man had shaken his resolve, and, if anything, he would use Sara to make his most chilling statement yet.

"You will be given the choice. By now, you know freedom can be yours if you choose to unleash the beast that resides in your soul. If you choose against freedom, a bullet is waiting for you."

Sara felt a sob rise in her throat. She fought it back down. She knew she had to stay focused, knew she couldn't allow her emotions to get the best of her. The others had died because they'd broken. Even stolid Brian Dennison had cracked when the Accuser had pressed hard. If she had any hope to stay alive, she had to keep her head.

Just stay calm. Just stay calm.

Sara's eyes met the young man's again. His gaze hadn't wavered, his calm, clear eyes hadn't moved from Sara's face. She knew then that she would fix her eyes on his, that his peaceful countenance would keep her centered.

Just look at him—keep your eyes on him…

The Accuser took his hand from her shoulder and leveled the gun at her head. His thin lips raised into his patented sneering smirk.

"Sara Thompson, I accuse you of being guilty of a terrible sin, one so foul and wretched that you are unworthy to still be among the living. You may choose freedom or death. What will you choose?"

***

SARA's breath caught in her throat as she heard the words that would eventually seal her doom.

"You may choose freedom or death. What will you choose?"

The Accuser placed his gun against Sara's temple. She knew her time was short. She'd have to start speaking or face immediate death.

"What is it going to be, Sara? Freedom or death? You have thirty seconds to decide."

Sara's heart rate accelerated. She knew her greatest sin. No soul-searching was necessary, no sifting through sins to find the most heinous one. The Accuser was right about the fact that her secret sin was foul enough for her to warrant death.

I've never told anyone…

The sin she harbored was so dirty, so *filthy*, she had vowed to herself never to speak it out loud. And she hadn't. How the

Accuser knew—and she knew that he knew—what her terrible secret was, she had no idea. He seemed to specialize in sin, seemed to feed off the suffering and errors of others.

I have to tell it. I have to or he'll kill me...

Sara took a deep, unsteady breath.

"I choose—freedom."

The Accuser's eyes danced in maniacal triumph.

"Good for you, Sara. You've chosen wisely. Now, please tell us all your most secret sin."

Sara's eyes found the young man's again, and she took another deep breath.

After you tell them, you'll be free...

"Okay. I was—I was a sophomore in high school ..."

Part II
Confession

Four years prior

Chapter Six

SARA JAMMED HER HISTORY BOOK INTO HER LOCKER and slapped the locker door shut. She'd had it with the drama, had it with the texts, had it with the stares. As she weaved her way through the oncoming traffic of the sophomore hallway, she felt her eyes well with familiar hot tears.

Don't cry here! If you cry here, they win! Just get to the bathroom!

Her iPhone buzzed in her pocket as she passed the science labs and the study hall room. It was hard to see through a bleary film of tears, and she twice ran into fellow classmates who mumbled curse words under their breath and went back to their fury-thumbed texting. She hated Infinity High School, hated the people who populated it, hated what it had done to her. One minute she had been its golden child, the next...

Just get to the bathroom! Don't cry here!

"Watch where you're going!" Meg Hurley said as Sara clipped her shoulder as the two passed. Sara pretended not to hear what Meg whispered under her breath.

"Slut!"

Sara could hold the tears back no longer. This was her life now. This was who she was. When you attended a small-town high school where the walls had ears and everyone knew everyone else's business, there was no escaping being categorized as *someone* or *something*. She couldn't escape what she was labeled; her cattle-branded scarlet letter was exposed for the entire high school to see. As she turned a corner and saw the blessed decal for the women's restroom, she wondered if it was better for her to just end it all. At least in death she'd find peace.

At least in death she'd find freedom.

***

SARA splashed some cold water on her face and wiped the smeared mascara from her cheeks. She was a hot mess. She prayed no one would come into the restroom to see what an emotional disaster she was. That was all she needed right now. She was already a pariah to the entire school. Whoever walked through that door wouldn't feel sorry for her. And she didn't blame them. She had made the decisions that had gotten her to this point. She had sealed her fate when she had taken that first fateful sip from the Solo cup she had reluctantly accepted at Valerie Frank's party.

It was her fault.

It was her shame.

It was her problem.

You don't deserve to live. You know it...

The familiar voices inside her head, the ones that had crept in after the events at the party, swirled in her brain like poison. The voices that degraded her, derided her, destroyed her, sounded like her own voice, but they were also so foreign. She had never known her subconscious was capable of such scathing self-indictments. She had never known she could hate herself so much.

You are a slut. You know it, they know it...

Sara looked at herself in the mirror through tear-bleary eyes. She used to be pretty—beautiful, even. Maybe she still was, but she didn't see it. Her shoulder-length blonde hair seemed overrun by split ends; her once bright, blue eyes seemed dimmer, duller. Her high cheekbones and slender face seemed ten years older, and the creases below her eyes screamed of insomnia and bone-weariness. Her body was all wrong—broken and worn, *used*. The dirtiness she felt inside had somehow seeped through her pores, and now she was contaminated. There was no undoing the past. There was no hiding from her present. And she saw no hope for a future.

You are nothing but used goods and you know it…

***

Eight Weeks Prior

"You have to go. *Everyone* will be there," Ashley said, plopping down on Sara's bed.

"Really? You're going to use that line on me? Is *everybody* really going to be there? Like, *everyone*?" Sara stepped out from her closet and held up two pairs of jeans. "Keep, or pitch?"

Ashley crinkled her nose. "Two thousand three called and wants its boot-cut jeans back. Pitch the pair in your left hand, keep the ones in your right. And, to be clear, when I say keep, I mean donate them to some organization that provides clothing to third-world countries."

Sara raised an eyebrow and nodded at the pair Ashley had labeled over a decade old. "I can't donate these?"

"If I were teenager in a third-world country, I'd rather go pantsless than wear those things."

Sara threw the pair of jeans at Ashley, who caught them and tossed them to the floor.

"Harsh, Ash. Harsh."

"You're trying to distract me with your subpar choices in clothing," Ashley said, lying back on the mattress. "You can clean out your closet some other time. Now we need to talk about you and Greg Daniels."

Sara felt her face flush. She quickly returned to her closet and pushed hangers to the left and right to cover her embarrassment. She'd never been good at concealing things, and her best friend usually read her like a book, despite her best efforts.

"There's nothing with me and Greg Daniels," Sara said, absently studying a lavender tank top.

"Right. Come on, Sara. I know you guys have been texting. He just followed you on Twitter. I *know* things. You can't hide the truth from me."

Sara popped her head out of the closet. "Stalker much?"

Ashley quickly sat up straight. "Ha! There! See? You just confirmed it! He *is* texting you!"

Sara sighed and crossed the room to her desk. Pulling out her chair, she sat down.

"So, what if I am texting Greg?"

Ashley's perfectly manicured eyebrows shot into her forehead.

"Do I really have to explain this to you, Sara? You're the honors student. But, if I must, I will speak slowly. Greg Daniels is—um—*super hot!* And, he's literally the most popular guy in Northwest Ohio. Literally, Sara. He's going to Ohio State on a full football scholarship. Quarterback. Hello, Sara, this guy is the complete package! Senior—quarterback—popular—hottie—hottie—hottie. Need I say more?"

She really didn't have to. Sara was fully aware of who and what Greg Daniels was. He was Infinity High School's prize possession. And the fact that he had even noticed Sara was extraordinary. He had set his books on the desk next to her in study hall, had sat down and smiled at her. He had dimples and gorgeous green eyes, tousled brown hair and arms that demanded to be admired. Sara had literally lost her breath when he'd spoken to her for the first time.

"You don't have to say anything more. I know who he is. I just—I don't know if I should go to the party."

"Um—*why not?*"

Sara picked up her iPod earbuds and absently untangled them as she spoke.

"I just turned sixteen. I'm a sophomore and it's an upperclassman party. And—there'll be alcohol."

Ashley laughed her off. "Really? Those are your objections? Um, I'm a sophomore and I just turned sixteen, too. And the legal drinking age is twenty-one, so everyone at the party will be breaking the law."

Sara rolled her eyes. "I guess if everyone is breaking the law that makes it okay."

"I get it that you want to be the goody-goody because it looks great on a college application. I don't blame you. You're uber-smart and you're going to get out of Northwest Ohio for whatever glorious career you choose. But, come on, Sara. You only get one time around in high school. Well— two if you're my stepbrother and you fail junior year. But, still. *Live* a little. Besides, I *know* you like Greg."

"And?"

"And he asked you to go. Don't you dare tell me he didn't, because you wouldn't want to lie through your teeth to your best friend. I know he asked you, because Derek asked me to go. And Derek's Greg's best friend, so—it's like, your destiny that you should go."

Sara finished untangling her iPod earbuds and placed them on her desktop.

"My destiny is to go to a party because you're playing tonsil hockey with the best friend of the guy I like?"

"See! Got you again! You like Greg. How can you *not*

43

like Greg? And, for your information, I'm not playing tonsil hockey with Derek. At least not more than four times."

"Oh. I forgot. It takes *five* times to make it a legit hockey match."

Ashley sighed. "You are too good at trying to weasel your way out of a conversation. Come on, Sara. One party. Just one. Who knows, maybe you'll even have enough fun to throw off your bonnet, hike up your *Little House on the Prairie* dress and let people do body shots off you as you flash a peace sign atop a pool table."

Sara couldn't help but grin and sigh. "Fine. I don't know how I let you talk me into things, but fine. I'll go. Happy now?"

Ashley flashed an exaggerated smile. "You know you love me. But not as much as you love Greg Daniels."

Sara shook her head. "You are shameless, you know that?"

***

SARA rubbed her eyes and glanced at her alarm clock. Sixteen after three in the morning. For some reason, her chemistry lab report wasn't coming together, and the stress of having to hand it in first period tomorrow morning—strike that, *this* morning—coupled with the tension from calculating how much sleep she wouldn't get, only served to muddle her brain more. And it wasn't as if she could just not do the lab report. Keeping her A in chemistry depended upon her turning the report in and doing well on it. She had to maintain her grade point average, had to stay number one in her class if she had even a snowball's chance in the hot place to get into Cornell.

Sara tossed her pen onto her desk next to her phone. Maybe she wouldn't be so tired if she hadn't texted Greg Daniels for two hours. She smiled and picked up her phone. Unlocking it, she thumbed through her conversation with Greg. There was no doubt he liked her. His flirtatiousness practically leapt through her iPhone's screen. And she couldn't deny that she liked him, too. And how couldn't she? Ashley had been right: Greg Daniels was the complete package of super-sexy athleticism and wit and charm that alone could turn heads. And that was why she knew she had to go to Valerie's party. She had no other option. If she wanted to be with Greg, she had to go to the places he went and do the things he did.

Sara set her phone down and leaned back in her chair. It finally seemed as if everything was clicking into place for her. For once, she felt as though she belonged at Infinity High School instead of belonging *to* Infinity High School. For so long she had been just the brainy girl with the right homework answers. Now, she was blossoming into a beautiful young woman—and people were starting to notice. The *right* people were starting to notice.

It feels good to belong...

Sara picked up her phone again. Was it too forward to text Greg now? He'd be asleep, for sure. But maybe she could just send him a good morning text so she would be the first thing he'd think about when he woke up.

No. That makes me seem desperate. It's three in the morning!

Her phone vibrated in her hand. When she saw whom the text was from, she could hardly contain her excitement.

I can't sleep. You still awake?

Maybe Ashley had been right about destiny. Maybe she and Greg were supposed to be together in some Disney princess, Prince Charming kind of way. She sat forward in her chair, placed her elbows on her desk, and thumbed back a response to the most popular boy in Northwest Ohio.

***

GREG Daniels smiled and his dimples became more prominent. It was all Sara could do not to sigh like a middle school girl.

"Do you need help with those books?" Gregg nodded at the bulky chemistry book she carried.

"I think I can manage, thanks," Sara said, trying hard to steady the pattering of her heart. This was all so new to her. To have a guy—and not just *any* guy, but Greg Daniels—take an interest in her was strange and exhilarating at the same time.

"I'm glad you're coming tomorrow night," Greg said, as he nodded hello to one of his football buddies. "Pick you up at eight?"

"Eight would be great," Sara said, immediately wanting to shove her foot into her mouth. Why was it her mind scrambled whenever Greg looked at her?

"Cute. Just like you. Hey, I have to get to English. Can I sit with you at lunch?"

You can ask me to marry you right now!

"Yeah. I'd like that." She tried to put on her most sincere yet slightly flirtatious smile.

Greg winked. "Good. Because I like you."

***

"SHUT up. Really? No—shut up!" Ashley said, pressing her lips together as she touched up her lipstick. She looked into the mirror, her eyes wide. Behind her, Sara couldn't help but smile.

"Yeah. He's sitting with us at lunch."

Ashley capped the lipstick and zipped it back into her purse.

"That's where you're wrong, dear. There's no *us* at lunch.

It's just you and the hottie."

Sara felt a mild panic rise in her chest. "You're ditching me?"

Ashley flipped her hair behind her shoulder, took one more glance at herself in the mirror, and turned around.

"It's for your own good. You and tight-butt need some alone time."

"Tight-butt?"

"Don't tell me you've never thought of cracking a walnut on that thing. Greg Daniels in football pants might be the best thing to ever happen to the universe."

Sara shook her head and rolled her eyes.

"You're lying if you say you've never checked out his butt."

Someone flushed the toilet in the second stall sending the girls into a giggling fit.

"What about you?" Ashley asked loudly. She giggled again as a sophomore girl Sara didn't know walked out of the stall.

"Greg Daniels? I'd watch him walk away all day."

Ashley playfully slugged Sara's arm as the girl washed her hands at one of the sinks.

"See? A girl can't help but stare."

"Okay. He has a great butt. But that doesn't mean you have to ditch me at lunch. What will we talk about?"

"What do you text about?"

The sophomore girl mercilessly pulled the paper towel dispenser's lever as Sara felt the panic continue to rise within her.

"Texting is different. I don't actually have to *see* him."

"Then pretend you don't see him. Strike that. He's gorgeous. See him."

Sara sighed. "I'm glad I can be your entertainment for the day."

"Come on, Sara. Does it really matter what you talk about? While you're sitting there eating with Greg you'll be the envy of every girl in school. He likes you, dear. He *likes* you."

Sara knew Ashley was right. Greg Daniels liked her—he had said as much in the hallway. And sitting alone with him at lunch would be a big step in the direction of a possible exclusive relationship between the football star and the bookish beauty.

Beauty might be a stretch...

"What if I say something stupid?"

"Just don't say anything stupid and you'll be fine."

Sara shook her head. "You know, you're not so great at pep talks."

"And you're not so great at figuring out social cues. Greg Daniels likes you, Sara, and that's all that matters. The rest will work itself out."

Sara sighed and looked at herself in the mirror.

"I hope you're right."

***

"No, seriously! Tell me! I promise I won't laugh!" Greg Daniels' eyes danced with playful mischief as he popped a Pringle into his mouth.

Sara blushed again. She might as well be permanently red considering all the times she had blushed since sitting down across from Greg at a circular table near the back of the cafeteria.

"No—it's—it's just a dumb nickname I had when I was a kid."

Greg's eyebrows shot into his forehead. "And it was?"

Sara shook her head. "Do you promise you won't laugh?"

"I already promise, but I'll promise to the fourth power,"

Greg said, raising his hand and holding the other atop the mound of muscle over his heart.

"Okay. It was—Twinkle Toes."

"*Twinkle Toes!*" Greg said, loudly.

"You don't have to announce it to the entire cafeteria!" Sara said, playfully swatting his right hand that now rested on the tabletop. She noticed a few people had turned to look at them, and she tried to pretend she didn't like being seen with Greg Daniels. The fact was she *loved* to be seen with Greg. She was the envy of every girl in the cafeteria. She'd seen them whispering, had seen the jealousy in their eyes. But *she* was the one with Greg. *She* was the one he wanted to be with.

"At least I didn't laugh," Greg said, smiling.

"Yeah. At least there's that."

Greg took a stick of celery from his lunch bag. "So, are you excited for Val's party?"

Sara didn't know what to say. Of course she was excited; she got to go with Greg. But she'd never experienced the fabled high school social gatherings. She had never had a beer, never so much as broken curfew. What did Greg expect of her?

"I—yeah. I'm excited."

Greg raised his eyebrows. "You don't sound too excited."

Sara sighed. "I guess I just—I've never had a drink before."

Greg's smile was back. Sara couldn't believe how his lips distracted her. Thin and perfectly pink, they screamed delicacy and suppleness. She'd never kissed a boy, and she was surprised to find herself thinking how much she'd love to know how soft his lips were.

"You don't have to drink. There'll be plenty of sober people there. Well, there should be a few. You don't have to do anything you don't want to do."

Sara felt she needed to explain herself. It wasn't that she

wanted to be lame, it was just that she didn't know how the party scene worked.

"I've just never been to a party like Val's before."

Greg reached across the table and put his hand over hers. The electricity that shot through her body made her heart flutter.

"You don't have to do anything you don't want to do, Sara. I'll be there to make sure of it."

Sara smiled, loving the warmth of his hand, the pronounced dimples of his cheeks.

"Okay. If you say so."

Greg winked. "I say so."

***

"You need something that screams sexiness," Ashley said, rummaging through Sara's closet. "Let me dig around a bit."

Sara sat on her bed, phone in hand. Greg had said he'd text her after football practice, and it was going on five thirty. He had texted her religiously the last few days, and she had come to expect her phone to vibrate an incoming message at about this time every evening. As she watched Ashley tear through her closet, Sara realized how pathetic it appeared. Here she was, the lovesick dame, clutching her phone in hopes her Prince Charming might send her a word. But even though it seemed ridiculous and like something Sara would've made fun of had she seen another girl do it, she couldn't help it. She had fallen for Greg something fierce. The very thought of him set her heart to a new kind of patter.

"Find anything?"

Ashley poked her head out of the closet long enough to roll her eyes.

"Your closet is like the wardrobe for an abstinence poster."

"Um—okay?"

Ashley squeaked some more hangers. "Seriously, Sara, it's a minor miracle that Greg even noticed you in the first place. The only thing missing in here is a chastity belt."

"I get it, Ash," Sara said, glancing at her phone. "My wardrobe is …"

"Straight out of 1955," Ashley finished, stepping out of the closet. She crossed the room and sat down beside Sara on the bed.

"I don't do the whole provocative thing," Sara said. Ashley patted her thigh.

"I'm only kidding. But, if you want, you can borrow something from my closet. We're about the same size."

Sara could hardly believe that was true. Just looking at Ashley and her lean, taut body and blonde hair, Sara couldn't grasp that she actually looked like Ashley. Since guys had started to notice her, Ashley had transformed herself into a stereotype. Sara would never tell her this, of course, but Ashley's fake tan and perfectly manicured nails made her seem less like herself and more like a caricature. She groomed her eyebrows every day and got pedicures at the place in the Toledo mall. She had even started talking differently, trying to hide her intelligence so she could fulfill the doe-eyed blonde persona she'd adopted since she had started dating Derek Johns. Where she had used to care about schoolwork and getting into Cornell with Sara, she now cared more about parties and making sure she never missed a day of ab and butt workouts. Sara missed the real Ashley. Or, perhaps, this was the real Ashley and Sara had never known it.

"So, what are you going to do if Greg kisses you?" Ashley asked, forgetting about Sara's apparently woeful wardrobe.

"Ash, I don't think he's going to."

"Come on, Sara. He's picking you up. You're going to Val's party, and then he has to *take you home*. You don't think he's going to kiss you?"

Sara's heartbeat accelerated. She'd thought of this scenario hundreds of times. In it, Greg walked her to her front door, leaned in to kiss her, and Sara met him halfway. And it was perfect. Beautiful. Hollywood couldn't write it any better. But that was merely fantasy. Reality was a much different matter.

"You're scared, aren't you?" Ashley asked. "You've never kissed a guy before, and you're nervous."

"Thanks for stating the obvious," Sara said.

Ashley laughed. "All you have to do is not think about it. Just go with the flow. Let him lead."

"There's some great advice," Sara said, grinning. "How does that help me?"

"It's not like kissing is rocket science. I mean, look how many dumb people manage to do it."

"Excellent point," Sara said, sarcastically. "Consider the fact that dumb people can kiss. That should make my experience all the better."

Ashley grabbed Sara's pillow and playfully hit Sara over the head.

"Stop. You know what I mean. It's easy. Have you ever thought about—you know—the other stuff?"

Sara looked at her best friend. "The other stuff?"

"Yeah. I mean, what if you guys start kissing, and one thing leads to another and …"

Sara grabbed the pillow and jammed it into Ashley's face. Ashley pulled it away and threw it to the side, laughing.

"Come on, Sara! I'm serious! What if it happens? Because it *can* happen."

"It's not going to happen," Sara said, glancing at her phone.

"Are you sure about that? I never thought it was going to happen, and …"

Sara looked at her friend, mouth agape. "What? What do you mean? You and Derek? You never—why didn't you tell me?"

Ashley took a deep breath, exhaled and shrugged. "It just happened. We were in his basement watching a movie. The lights were out and—yeah—it just happened."

Sara was speechless. Ashley was her best friend. They'd shared the most intimate conversations, knew things about each other no other soul on the planet knew. And now Ashley was shrugging off a monumental life moment like this?

"I—I don't know what to say, Ash," Sara said.

"See? That's why I didn't tell you," Ashley said softly. "I didn't want you to judge me."

"I'm not judging you. It's just—we're best friends. We tell each other everything, and you didn't tell me about this."

"I'm sorry, Sara. I just—it just happened."

Sara nodded, unsure of what to say next. She had so many questions, some about why Ashley would keep such a thing a secret, and some about the experience itself.

"If you want to know the truth, it wasn't all that exciting," Ashley said. "At least not the first time."

Sara trod lightly. She could sense the tension in the subject, and she didn't want to scare Ashley away from the conversation. Her best friend already thought Sara would judge her.

"There was more than one time?"

"Sex is like crack cocaine to the male species," Ashley said, smiling. "One hit isn't enough."

Sara didn't know how to respond, so she didn't.

"I mean, we're safe about it. I got the pill a few days ago."

Sara just nodded, not having any idea what to say. This was foreign territory. They had turned a page in their friendship, had gone from the children's chapters to the adult ones, and Sara was still adjusting to the new setting.

"Say something, Sara," Ashley said. "Just—tell me you're okay with it. You're my best friend, and I need that confirmation from you."

Sara didn't know whether she was okay with it. She didn't know a lot of things these days. She seemed to be morphing and changing into somebody new with each passing day. She had never expected to fall for Greg Daniels, had never expected to be going to a party like Val's. And she certainly hadn't expected to be having such a conversation with her best friend. Time was speeding up. Things were happening so quickly now. Maybe that's what happened during your teenage years, and maybe it was perfectly normal. Yet Sara couldn't help but feel she wanted to apply the brakes a little, to slow down life and all these experiences so she could think clearly about them instead of just acting in the moment.

"As long as you're happy, so am I," Sara said, squeezing Ashley's knee.

Her best friend looked at her, and Sara could see a trace of sadness in her eyes.

"I'm happy. Derek is awesome. And so is Greg. You need to think about these kinds of things, Sara. You never know what will happen when one thing leads to another."

"I do know, though," Sara said softly. "I know that I'm—I'm going to save myself."

Ashley laughed. "You sound like Christine Meadows! Like one of those other Christian prudes!" She sat up straight and assumed a nasally, self-righteous voice. "'I'm going to save myself for marriage. It will be glorious. My husband shall carry me across the threshold, and we shall lie together in a bed of roses.'"

Sara couldn't help but laugh. Ashley *did* sound like Christine Meadows, Infinity High School's uber-Christian in residence.

"I didn't judge you, Ash!"

Ashley put her hand in the air. "Okay, okay. Sorry. I was just kidding. I won't judge you. If that's how you want to go about it, it's your life. But I'm putting money on the fact that half those girls who go around saying they're saving themselves are the ones who are the freakiest behind closed doors."

Sara laughed. "You're awful, do you know that?"

Ashley placed her finger to her lips and pretended to look around the room.

"Sshh. I don't want Christine Meadows sending me to hell."

Sara picked up the pillow again and threw it at her best friend. Ashley caught it and continued laughing.

Sara laughed along with her. But deep down in her heart of hearts, Sara knew she sided more with Christine Meadows on the subject than she did with Ashley. But she could never tell her best friend that, and never would. Especially now that Ashley and Derek were making a routine of it.

I won't have to worry about it, anyway. Greg's not like that.

***

"THAT's an—interesting choice," Sara's mother said, sipping from a steaming mug of green tea. She assessed the short blue skirt Ashley had allowed Sara to borrow, took in the white spaghetti-strapped top, which was also Ashley's.

"What, Mom?" Sara asked. She crossed the kitchen and took a glass from the cupboard. She didn't really have to question why her mother thought her get-up was 'interesting' because she herself felt incredibly uncomfortable. The skirt was entirely too short, and the top had a dangerously low cut. She felt out of her element and completely as if she was wearing someone else's clothes. But Ashley had insisted she looked great in the blue skirt and white top, so Sara had agreed to wear the outfit. Now she was having second thoughts.

"It's just something that's outside your norm," her mother said, closing the book she was reading on her iPad. She set her mug on the kitchen table as Sara turned on the tap and waited for the water to chill.

"Well, my norm is getting a little too normal," Sara said, filling her glass. "I'm just trying to expand my horizons."

Her mother grinned. She was a pretty woman with acorn-brown hair and the same facial features as Sara: high cheekbones, dark eyes, a forehead that seemed just a smidgen too broad.

"Has your father seen your attempt at expanding your horizons yet?"

Sara took a drink. When she raised the glass, she couldn't keep from trembling. She was beyond nervous. Greg would be here at any moment and the night would begin.

"No. He's in the den on the computer."

"He'll want to meet Greg when he gets here," her mother said. "We've certainly read enough about him in the newspaper. Quite an athlete."

Sara hoped her mother would make her go change. She didn't want to wear Ashley's clothes to the party. Her own clothes would make her feel so much more comfortable.

"I'm sure he'll hear the doorbell," Sara said, placing her glass in the sink.

"Dishwasher, please."

Sara took the glass out of the sink and opened the half-full dishwasher.

"Just say it, Mom. Do you think what I'm wearing is inappropriate?"

Please, tell me it is.

Her mother looked her up and down again. "I've seen

much worse, dear. Have fun tonight. What movie are you seeing again?"

Sara hadn't dared to tell her parents she was going to a senior party where there'd be alcohol. Ashley had instructed her to tell her parents Greg was taking her out to dinner and then to the putt-putt golf course in Lewiston, with a late movie to follow. This plan had gotten her dad to extend her curfew by an hour but brought with it the shame of lying to her parents.

"Uh—it's the new Marvel superhero movie. I'm not sure what it's called, but Greg's been dying to see it, so I told him it was okay as long as I got two chick-flicks at a later date out of the deal."

Her mother laughed, and Sara felt terrible. "I've raised you well."

Her mother's words were a punch to the gut. She *had* raised Sara well. Well enough to know that the scheme she and Ashley had concocted was deceitful.

"What can I say? The apple doesn't fall too far from the tree."

The doorbell rang and Sara felt all the blood drain from her face.

"I believe your chariot awaits," her mother said, standing. She set her mug of tea on the kitchen table and walked around the kitchen island to Sara. She put her arm around Sara's shoulder and kissed her cheek.

"My baby's all grown up. One day you're in diapers, the next you're going on a date with Ohio State's future quarterback."

The doorbell sounded again, and Sara heard her father's muffled footsteps on the hardwood floor.

"I was hoping to get to the door before Dad," Sara said. Her mother kissed her again.

"I love you. Be safe, okay?"

"Okay, Mom."

Sara willed her heartbeat to slow down as she exited the kitchen. Her father had already opened the front door and was welcoming Greg inside.

"Come on in, Greg. Sara should be—oh, here she is."

Her father's eyes widened as he took in her outfit. As badly as she wanted to shuck the garb in favor of her own clothes, she hoped against hope that her father wouldn't embarrass her in front of Greg.

"I was just letting Greg in," her father said, making eyes at his wife in relation to Sara's outfit. Sara knew there would be a long talk tomorrow. That was assuming he actually let her out of the house wearing this outfit in the first place. "Hey, Sara," Greg said, smiling. His All-American dimples were prominent, and the blue polo he wore brought out the deep green of his eyes.

"Hi."

Greg politely shook Sara's father's hand and then followed with her mother's.

"So, you're going to Ohio State next year," her father said. As an avid Buckeye fan, her dad was probably more excited than she was that she was going on a date with Greg.

"Yeah. Finally decided Columbus is where I want to be. I thought about Iowa for a bit, but I couldn't pass up a chance to play for the team I've grown up rooting for."

"As long as you were never considering That Team Up North, you are welcome to take my daughter out tonight," her father said, clapping Greg's shoulder.

"I wasn't that desperate to play college football," Greg answered on cue.

Sara's father erupted in laughter. "You are a wise man, Greg."

"We extended Sara's curfew by an hour so you guys can see the late movie," Sara's mother said.

Greg's eyes flashed to Sara and then back to her mother. He didn't miss a beat, even though Sara hadn't let him in on her scheme. She assumed he had cooked up a similar scheme with his own parents, so the particulars of hers didn't matter. Being a novice at concocting devious plans to attend high school beer bashes, Sara hadn't considered that Greg might actually have to face his parents, and that it was, indeed, important for him to know her scheme.

"Thanks. I hope that's not a problem," Greg said, charm oozing from his voice.

He's done this before.

"As long as you promise to beat Michigan the four years you're at OSU," her father answered.

"Five years. I'm going to redshirt my first season. But, absolutely. I'll make sure of it just for you."

Sara's father beamed. He was enjoying this too much.

"You kids have fun," Sara's mother said, squeezing her shoulder.

"Thanks, Mrs. Thompson," Greg said. He shook Sara's father's hand one more time, and then opened the front door and motioned for Sara to go first.

As she walked out her front door, Sara felt as if she were making a mockery of her parents' trust. And, strangely, it didn't feel as bad as she thought it would.

***

"So, what movie are we supposedly going to see tonight?" Greg asked when they were both safely strapped into his Mustang. He pulled away from the curb in front of her house and looked over at her. His boyish grin and predominant dimples were almost too much.

"Are you mad?" Sara asked, nervous that she had already botched the night.

Greg laughed. "Of course not. I just need to make sure I Google a synopsis of the plot so I can at least hold my own if we're questioned about it. You should probably do the same at some point."

"I told them it was that new superhero movie—the Marvel one."

"Good! For a second there I thought I'd have to read up on a chick flick."

"Maybe next time," Sara said, immediately regretting her words. Who said there would even be a next time?

Greg nodded as he took a right onto Franklin Street. "Yeah. Maybe next time." He looked at her again. "You look beautiful, by the way."

Sara felt the warm flush rise to her cheeks. "Thanks. It's a little out of my element."

"I know. And you make it look good."

Sara could barely believe this was happening. How could she, a bookish, grade-conscious geek, really be sitting in the passenger seat of Greg Daniels' car? It all seemed so surreal, so *weird*.

"Thank you. You look pretty handsome yourself."

Greg smiled, reached over the console and gave Sara's bare knee a squeeze.

"Ready for a great night?"

She looked at Greg's hand as it lingered on her knee. The warmth of his palm, the skin-on-skin contact, disoriented her. She placed her hand over his.

"I'm up for anything."

***

"You look *hot*," Ashley said as she met Sara on the sidewalk leading up to Valerie Frank's sprawling house. Greg and Derek were walking close behind them, talking about one of the Top Plays they had seen on *Sportscenter*.

"I feel ridiculous in this skirt," Sara whispered back, tugging at the bottom of the skirt.

"Trust me. You look hot in it. Whoever gave it to you must have impeccable taste." Ashley pushed a strand of her blonde hair behind her ear. She wore a much-too-tight and much-too-short pink dress that accentuated the liquid flow of her body. Only last year, she and Sara had whispered nasty things about girls who wore dresses like Ashley's. Now Ashley was the one wearing the dress. How quickly things changed.

"Where are her parents?" Sara asked as they stepped onto the front porch.

Ashley laughed. "Does it matter? Remember, let yourself have some fun. This isn't a study group. No grade is riding on this. Have. Some. Fun. Okay?"

Sara felt Greg's hand on the small of her back. When she turned her head to look at him, he was smiling. "Ready?"

She took a deep breath and smiled back. "Ready."

"Good. Let's have some fun."

***

THE first thing Sara noticed was that everyone who was anyone at Infinity High School was sprinkled around Valerie Frank's expansive and expensive living room and kitchen. They were the upperclassmen movers and shakers, the upper crust who kept Infinity High School on the map. They all sipped from red Solo cups as they laughed and flirted. Valerie's parents' house provided a fantastic venue for them to mingle, with its open floor plan and vast array of leather furniture. The living room was four times bigger than Sara's and painted with contemporary greens accented by mochas and dark browns. The living room opened into a kitchen filled with stainless steel appliances, expensive countertops and crisp, white cupboards. The décor was the first thing Sara noticed.

The second thing Sara noticed was that everyone was staring at her.

This was a mistake. I shouldn't have come.

Sara felt the warmth of Greg's hand on the small of her back again. She couldn't deny it was a little reassuring, but she still felt like a spectacle on display in her short skirt and low-cut top.

"Geez. Stare much?" Ashley whispered as she squeezed Sara's arm. "They're harmless, I promise."

"They're just admiring how beautiful you look," Greg said, flashing his dimpled smile.

Sara smiled back, still very much aware of the stares and whispers. She wished she could believe Greg, but deep down she knew she was being sized up and assessed. She was Greg Daniels' new girl, and they were trying to determine how and why she was worthy of his eye.

"I'm going to get a drink," Ashley said. "I'll let you and Greg make the rounds. Coming, Derek?"

As Sara watched her best friend and boyfriend weave through the clumps of upperclassmen, she felt helplessly out of place. Yet, there was an excitement behind the nervousness that was downright thrilling.

Relax. Enjoy yourself. You're only young once.

A tall blonde wearing a low-cut white top and a pencil skirt made her way to Greg and Sara. Sara knew the blonde who seeped sexuality and walked with liquid grace was Valerie Frank. Sara had heard rumors about how Valerie had slept with the Infinity High School football team's entire starting defense and was working her way through the offense. Sara knew it probably wasn't true, but she also knew that every high school rumor carried a shred of truth, no matter how small the shred was. So, when Valerie extended her hand to Sara, all Sara could think about was Valerie's love of touch football.

"You're Sara, right?" Valerie smiled as Sara shook her hand. "I don't think we've ever met. I'm Val."

Val, not Valerie. Being with Greg already has me shortening popular girls' names.

"Yeah, I don't think we've met," Sara said, not really knowing what to say. "You have a beautiful house."

"You're too nice," Val said, flipping a hand at Sara. "It's a big house and it's great for parties. Especially when your dad takes frequent international business trips and your mom's out of the picture."

Sara only nodded politely.

Val winked at Greg and took a sip from her cup. "You've outdone yourself this time, Greggy."

Greg laughed and Sara tried to ignore the familiarity in Val's voice. She hadn't considered until this very moment that Val and Greg could have a history that extended into the bedroom. She shook off the thought as self-doubt threatened to overtake her. She really didn't belong here, but she'd *learn* to belong with these people.

Greggy...

"Well, Greg, you know the drill. Keg's in the garage; stay out of my dad's den and bedroom."

"Always good to be reminded," Greg said. He turned to Sara. "Shall we?"

Sara took Greg's extended hand, her heart pounding. She smiled. "We shall."

Greg led her through the living room and the sea of popular people parted as though he were Moses. He slapped hands with multiple boys Sara only knew from awed female whispers in study hall and in the girl's locker room. Sara's cheeks hurt from smiling. She felt like the First Lady; she was with the most popular boy in the county—and in a few years, when he quarterbacked for Ohio State, the most popular boy in the *state*—and all she could think about was how she was a goldfish trapped in a bowl with a roomful of gawkers far above her social status.

"Gotta get to the garage," Greg said, leading her into the kitchen. The pair walked around the immaculate kitchen island and headed for a door on the west wall. When Greg opened it for her, Sara realized there were, essentially, two parties happening at once. The tamer variety occupied Val's living room, and the rowdier was taking place in the ridiculously huge four-car garage.

"Keg's over there," Greg said, head-nodding to a group of slightly-less-popular juniors than those who occupied the living room. "It's loud in here. Wow."

Greg's assessment of the garage's decibel condition was more than slightly understated. The place was a veritable zoo of drunken shouting, coarse language and squeaking sneakers. The sound reverberated off the walls of the cavernous space, and Sara realized that this spectacle was what teen party movies were based off. Every person sipped from a blue or red Solo cup, and as she looked around, she was confident that those who made up the scene were considered second-tier popular. These were the noblemen and noblewomen of Infinity High School's feudal system, while the kings and queens occupied the Franks' living room. She knew without even having been to a party like this that Greg's presence in the garage was only temporary.

"The beer's not great," Greg said as he led her to a silver keg sitting along the wall. "I'm pretty sure it's Natty Light."

Sara didn't know Budweiser from Heineken, so Natty Light meant nothing to her. All she knew was that she was expected to drink it and smile.

"I'll get you a cup. Red or blue for my lady?" Greg smiled

and Sara's heart galloped.

"Red, please."

"Red it is."

Sara watched as Greg filled her cup from the keg's tap. She wondered if anyone ever actually did a keg stand like she'd seen in the movies. When Greg handed her the cup, Sara surveyed the foaming contents.

Greg filled his cup, took a sip and nodded at Sara. "You've never had a beer, have you?"

"It's that obvious, huh?"

Greg laughed. "You don't have to drink it if you don't want to."

Everything within her screamed for her to put the cup down, to give the beer back to Greg and remain sober and clearheaded. A warning strobed in the back of her mind, a premonition of something terrible to come if she accepted the drink.

Come on, Sara. Don't be a wuss. You're only young once.

The warning in her head turned into a siren's wail. She closed her mind to it, willed herself to block it out.

I'm going to have fun. Besides, it's just one beer.

Sara raised her cup. "To us."

Greg laughed again. "Wow. Way too formal for Natty Light, but I'll drink to that."

Sara smiled, raised her arm toward her lips and sipped from the cup that would destroy her life forever.

***

"How's my girl?" Ashley stepped away from a group of seniors and sloppily hugged Sara. Beer sloshed over the rim of Ashley's cup and onto the white carpet of the living room floor. Sara's beer-foggy mind tried to comprehend how expensive the Franks' carpet must be. Probably imported from some small European country no one had ever heard of and made from the fur of an exotic mammal recently added to the endangered species list. At any rate, Ashley hadn't realized she had spilled her beer, and now she clumsily wrapped an arm around Sara's shoulders. Greg was talking to a group of his friends a few feet away, and for the first time that evening, Sara felt comfortable enough to stand alone in the room of Infinity High School's movers and shakers. Chalk it up to liquid courage or whatever you wanted, but Sara's confidence was on the rise. And that was a good feeling, one very different from the feeling she'd had upon her arrival at the party.

"Living while I'm young," Sara said, raising her cup.

"That's what I'm talking about!" Ashley's voice was much too loud for their close proximity. "So, you and Greg?"

"Me and Greg, what?"

Ashley lifted her precisely manicured eyebrows up and down twice. "He make a move?"

Sara laughed, both at Ashley's question and at the slur of her words.

"What makes you think he'll make a move?"

"He's a teenage boy who's never been shut down by a girl. Trust me, the move is coming."

Sara surveyed the scene in the living room. "Here? No way. And, besides, who says I want him to make a move?"

Ashley looked at Sara as if Sara were the dumbest person alive. "Okay. Listen. If a guy like Greg likes you, he'll make a move wherever. And, do I *even* have to respond to you not *wanting* him to make a move? You may be a Puritanical prude, but when Greg gets close enough to kiss you, with those eyes and those dimples—even *you* will give in."

"Puritanical prude, huh?"

Ashley laughed much too loudly. "Well, you aren't dressed like one tonight. Girl, your legs are downright scandalous!"

Sara felt a warmth on the small of her back. Ashley disentangled herself from Sara's shoulders and smirked at her as Greg sidled close.

"How's my girl?"

Sara couldn't help it. Her heartbeat accelerated.

His girl?!

"I was just telling her how great she looks tonight," Ashley said, still smirking.

"She looks amazing," Greg said, his eyes shining, his dimples creating perfect divots in his cheeks. Ashley had been completely right. His eyes and dimples were even more intoxicating than the alcohol.

"I'll leave you two alone," Ashley said. She winked at Sara and made her way back to Derek's group of friends.

Greg laughed. "What was that all about?"

"Just Ashley being Ashley."

"Yeah, she's had quite the—what's that big word that means change?"

"Metamorphosis?" Sara supplied.

"Right. Metamorphosis. Here I thought I'd go and dispel the myth that football players are dumb as cinderblocks and I bungled the word." He pressed closer to her and she could feel the heat of his side against hers.

"You're the quarterback, right? Aren't quarterbacks supposed to be the smartest guys on the field?"

"Sara Thompson, you know football?"

Sara laughed. "I watch with my Dad on Saturdays. Sometimes on Sundays."

Greg put his arm around her shoulders. "Marry me now."

Sara couldn't help but laugh giddily. How had this happened? How had she gone from bookish nerd to being fake-proposed to by the most popular boy in the county?

"Aren't we moving a little too quickly?"

Greg's voice was buttery with sexiness.

"We can move as quickly as you like."

***

HER eyeballs felt like Civil War musket balls in their sockets. Every time she moved them they felt so heavy.

It's just part of it.

Even her thoughts seemed to come from the other room. Her head was heavy yet felt like helium, and her cheeks and the tip of her nose tingled. As she tried to concentrate on what Val Frank was saying to her, she felt Greg's hand pressing on the upper swell of her butt.

"And so I told her to back off my man," Val said loudly, her words slurring together. For the life of her Sara couldn't remember who Val's man had been and why Val had told him off. But Greg found it hilarious, his boisterous laugh indicating as much. He slammed back against the back of the leather couch clutching his stomach with his left hand while keeping his right on Sara's backside. Val erupted into messy laughter, and Sara took her cue and did the same.

Greg sucked the last of his beer from his blue cup and shook it back and forth.

"Crap. I'm out." The realization he was now beerless struck him as funny, and he burst into another fit of laughter.

"You out, too, Greg?" Tyson Francis, another uber-popular football player, asked as he walked by the couch. He stopped and extended his hand. "Here, I'm going to the garage. I'll fill you up." He looked at Sara. For some reason Tyson's glassy eyes sent a chill down her spine. It was probably just the alcohol, but Tyson's eyes seemed almost evil.

Stop it! He's harmless!

Sara handed her cup to Tyson. "Sure, I'll have another."

Sara was surprised at the sound of her own voice. She sounded sleep-dopey and slurry. How many beers had she had?

"Coming right up," Tyson said, quickly weaving his way through the crowd on his way to the garage.

"Thanks, bro!" Greg called after him. Sara felt his thumb caress her butt as he looked at her with distant eyes. "Having fun?"

Sara realized for the first time that if Greg was drunk, he wouldn't be able to drive her home. She certainly couldn't drive Greg's Mustang. She couldn't drive a stick, and the prospect of even walking to the door felt hazardous. She'd consumed five—or was it six?—beers, and even though she had no idea what being drunk felt like, she knew she was two beers away from being obliterated. All of these thoughts floated in her mind, but she couldn't grab hold of them to make clear sense of any of them.

"I'm having a blast."

Greg smiled. "I am too. You're awesome."

And before Sara knew what was happening, his lips were moving over hers. Even though her lips tingled with excess alcohol consumption, the sensation that shot through her body was electrifying. When Greg finally pulled away, her head spun not only from the drinks, but also from the euphoria of her first kiss.

Greg winked. "More later?"

"Yeah," Sara breathed. The electricity continued to sizzle through her body. She wanted him to kiss her again, to feel his body on hers. The feelings were all so new, so amazing, that Sara didn't know what would happen if she got the chance to be with Greg alone.

"OMG! Get a room!" Val said, laughing. "You two are too cute!"

Tyson Francis' voice cut through the moment. "Here's your beer, man." He handed Greg his cup and then turned to Sara. "And here's a special one just for you."

Another chill snaked its way down Sara's spine. She looked at her cup. It was the same one she had been sipping from the whole night. She knew as much because she had nibbled on the top and the tiny indentations of her teeth were embedded in the plastic. Still, something felt wrong.

It's nothing. Just take the drink and get on with the night.

"Thanks." She took the cup as Tyson's lips spread into a smirk.

"You did well with this one, Greg." He slapped Greg on the back and Greg laughed, not noticing the wink Tyson gave her as he walked away.

Sara watched Tyson walk away and heard the sirens go off in her head again.

Forget about him. Just have fun.

Sara felt Greg's hand squeeze her bottom, and all the warning sirens melted away. She took a sip from her beer and tried to follow a story Val was telling about a prank she'd pulled in middle school. But she couldn't focus on Val. All she could think about was how Greg's lips had felt against hers, and about how much she wanted to feel them again.

***

There was light and then there wasn't. There were whispers that resolved into silence. There was warmth, weight, hot air on her cheek. Everything was fractured. Her world was blips. Nothing linear. Just blips.

"Sshh...it's okay..."

There was pressing, there was scratching. There was softness on her back. There was searing pain.

Blips.

Blips.

Blips.

"She's completely wasted..."

The sirens in her head wailed. They blared.

They blared.

They blared…

"Sshh…just let me…"

There was skin on her skin. There were hands around her wrists. Everything was blips.

Blips.

"Sara, what are you doing!"

Blips.

"She's not a good girl anymore."

Blips.

"Sshh…not so loud."

And then, nothing.

***

SOMEONE was jamming an icepick into the core of her brain. Her whole body ached; her stomach, her wrists. Her lower torso felt ripped in half, and panic swept over her as she opened her eyes.

What is going on?

Sara raised her head and felt an explosion in her brain. Little blips of light floated in her vision, dancing in the morning light that streamed through the blinds of her bedroom.

My bedroom?!

A slow, terrible realization washed over her.

I—I can't remember anything!

She sat bolt upright in her bed and felt her body curse her for her effort. How had she gotten home?

I was so drunk I don't remember anything.

She was wearing Ashley's dress from the party, and when she brought her hands to her face to try to rub off some of the confusion, she saw angry bruises on both her wrists.

What—happened?

For the first time, real fear stabbed her like a knife. She realized she could only remember bits and pieces of the previous night, and nothing after she and Greg had been talking on Valerie's couch. Why had her memory gone into hibernation? How could she not remember anything beyond that point?

The first sob came and she sucked it back into her throat. She couldn't cry. Not now, anyway. She didn't want to alert her parents to the fact that she had come home drunk and had passed out, fully dressed, on her bed. She had to call Ashley. Ashley would tell her what had happened last night.

Sara's phone was on the bed beside her. Thankfully she hadn't misplaced it in her drunken state. Clicking on the screen, she looked at the time. Seven after eight o'clock. Ashley would probably be sleeping off her drunken night, but Sara didn't care. She had to know what had happened last night. She had to know why there were bruises on her wrists and why the core of her felt as if it had been torn apart like notebook paper. Carefully shifting her body on her mattress, she started to dial Ashley's number. The short skirt rode up a little, and she pushed herself up to pull it down a bit.

That's when she saw the lines of dried blood on her inner thighs.

***

THE shower spray felt like acid on her skin as her tears mixed with the assaulting water and swirled down the drain. She couldn't get clean, couldn't wash off the filth she felt clinging to her skin.

She was dirty.

She had been used.

She had been *raped*.

Sara tried to swallow a sob that threatened to escape her

lips. She couldn't let her parents know about what had happened, not yet, anyway. Not until she herself knew what had transpired. Her body rocked with the sobs she kept inside her as she pulled her legs tighter to her herself in a seated fetal position.

What now? What do I do?

Sara knew she should go to the emergency room. She knew doctors would bring out a rape kit and confirm what she already knew to be true. But the immediate reality of the situation, the surreal horror of it, kept her silent in the shower. Going to the emergency room would only exacerbate the problem. If she went to the emergency room and they found that she had, indeed, been violated, as she knew she had been, the police would get involved. And then all hell would break loose for those who'd been at the party, Val's parents, *her* parents and who knew who else. She knew she had to make a decision quickly and that her decision had the potential to destroy more lives than her own. That's what it came down to, really. She had to determine whether her life was more valuable than everyone else's involved.

You know the answer to that, Sara. It's not even worth debating. You are a forgettable loser.

The voices in her head assaulted her like the shower's spray. She was damned either way. At least one other person knew she'd been raped, and that was the person who had raped her. But what if that got out? What would happen to her at school? What if her parents discovered the truth? And what about Greg?

Greg...

Had it been Greg Daniels? Had he drunkenly forced himself on her? Had he taken advantage of the fact that she'd never consumed alcohol before and couldn't possibly comprehend the full ramifications of her heavy drinking? Sara's body rocked with another sob as she thought about it. No, it couldn't have been Greg. Greg wasn't like that. Greg was different from most guys. Wasn't he?

Isn't he?

The water instantly turned ice cold. Sara had no idea how long she'd been sobbing in the shower, but the hot water had been replaced by a biting cold spray. She shivered against it, but she didn't move. She didn't deserve to move. This was all her fault. She should have known what she was doing, should have kept her inhibitions.

It's your fault. You were raped, and it is your fault because you didn't know your limit.

And then a thought that shook her to the core:

What if I'm pregnant?

Her brain cannoned with pain and horror. No. No way. This couldn't be happening to her. She was Sara Thompson, future Cornell grad. She had her whole life ahead of her. And now it had the potential to be ripped away from her because she had allowed herself to be violated by a nameless boy at a high school beer bash.

I have to call Ashley. She has to know something...

But even as she thought it, Sara knew no one else could save her from her situation. She was in it alone. And as the frigid water beat down on her, she wondered for the first time if life could ever be worth living again.

***

SARA shivered as she picked up her phone. Even the hoodie and sweats she'd thrown on couldn't ward off the trembling, and she knew the shower's frigid spray only accounted for a fraction of her tremors. She had been raped, and she had to find out all Ashley knew about last night. And, after that, she had to question Greg.

Her fingers robotically worked her iPhone. She touched

Ashley's number as her heart hammered in her chest. One ring, two.

"What?" Ashley's voice sounded annoyed and abrupt, and it stunned Sara to a momentary silence.

"Hello?"

Sara couldn't contain her tears. "Ash—what—what happened last night?"

Ashley sighed, and Sara heard disgust in Ashley's exhale. "I can't do this, Sara. Not now—not ever. I have a raging headache, and …"

Sara raised her voice to a dangerous level. The last thing she wanted was her parents bursting through the door, but she couldn't help it. Bleary tears stained her vision, and the snot freely flowed over her upper lip.

"Ashley! Please! What happened last night?"

"You know, you have a lot of nerve to act like you don't know. But I guess that fits the whole I'm-wholesome persona, doesn't it? You're just lucky I brought you home."

"*You* brought me home? What happ–"

Ashley's voice assumed a vicious whisper. "I don't want you to call me, text me—I don't want you to *look* at me at school!"

"Ashley—please—I think—I think I was raped."

To Sara's utter horror, Ashley laughed.

"Raped? *Raped?* Is that what you're going to call it? I can't believe you."

Sara shook with sobs. Confusion mixed with hangover pain inside her brain creating a muddled mess of oblivion.

"What are you talking about?"

Ashley laughed again, scorn dripping from her voice. "You *slut!* You screwed the *whole party!* You screwed my *boyfriend!* And now you're going to claim *you were raped!?*"

Sara nearly dropped the phone. Her knees gave out from underneath her, and she collapsed to the floor in a heap of confused terror.

"What—what …"

"*Never* talk to me again! *Never!* And if you act like a victim—if you even *think* about crying rape, I'll make sure you rot for it! I'll be the *first person* to testify against you!" Ashley was screaming now. "Do you hear me, *slut?!* Huh? Do you *hear me?!* You're not *a victim*! It's *your* fault! *Yours!*"

"Ashley—I don't know what—Ashley?"

But Ashley had already hung up. As her best friend's words exploded in her brain, Sara had never felt so alone, so *accused*. She crumpled onto the carpet, her body rocking with sobs. If what Ashley had said was true, Sara's life was over.

It's your *fault!*
It's YOUR *fault!*
Slut!
SLUT!

***

THE weeks that followed were pure hell. Sara walked the halls of Infinity High School as a pariah. The looks she received, the whispers, the blatant stares, caused her to miss four straight days with flu-like symptoms. She could tell no one what had happened, and yet everyone knew. They knew she had whored herself out to the male population at Valerie's party, knew she carried a scarlet letter on her soiled breast, knew she had been reduced to nothing more than a *slut*. She stopped doing her homework, and her grades plummeted. She stopped stepping out of the blessed sanctuary of her room when she was at home, and her parents grew concerned. But what could she tell them? They seemed to be the only two people on the planet who didn't know what had happened. In the middle of a few sleepless nights, when the demons of her own guilt hovered above her bed, she almost walked to their room and told them everything. Told them the *truth*. But she didn't do it—couldn't do it. Especially when she couldn't know with one hundred percent certainty that she had even been raped. After all, it was *her* fault for drinking herself into oblivion. They were *her* actions when she had been under the influence, even if they weren't coherent ones. If she'd had sex with a multitude of equally-drunk guys, did that mean they had raped her? Did that mean she was technically not responsible for what had happened?

But there was one cloying thought Sara couldn't shake: What if someone had slipped something into her drink while she was unaware? For some macabre reason, Sara actually hoped this theory held water. At least it would explain what had transpired. But she also knew she lived in rural Northwest Ohio and not in New York City, or even in the teenage world Hollywood depicted. Her peers didn't have access to date rape drugs, did they?

But Tyson Francis had taken my drink...

Sara had no one to blame but herself; and, as her life began to crumble around her, she realized she was utterly and irrevocably alone.

No one could save her. She wasn't worth being saved, anyway.

***

It wasn't until she missed her period that Sara seriously considered she might be pregnant. First she was one week late. And then two. And then the dread and unadulterated horror began to creep over her. She couldn't be pregnant—just couldn't be. Surely the boys who had taken advantage of her had at least worn protection. They couldn't have been *that* stupid. But even as she thought it, she knew that, yes, it was more than possible that one or more of the guys had been that stupid. Libido and alcohol were a wicked mixture. A horrifically wicked mixture.

For two days Sara hid in her room, first in denial, and then with the weight of certainty slithering around her being. The certainty was an anaconda wrapped around her body, slowly squeezing her, slowly constricting the life out of her. She was certain she was pregnant, certain that pregnancy, in this case, was worse than an STD. A few unsightly bumps and painful bouts of urination would be welcome in place of this. Pregnancy was a knife to the jugular of her self-worth, her reputation and her hopes and dreams.

I have to know for sure…

***

SARA unwrapped the stick from its protective package and placed it on the bathroom vanity countertop. Her heart was pounding; her knees felt like liquid beneath her. As she looked at herself in the mirror, she saw a tragedy looking back at her. Her eyes were hollow and sunken, her hair ratty and unkempt. Heavy bags rested underneath her eyes, and her skin sucked in around her once beautiful high cheek-bones. As she looked at herself in the mirror, the pregnancy test stick a white bomb on the vanity top, Sara wondered who would miss her if instead of peeing on the stick, she opened the veins of her wrists in the bathtub or fixed her neck tightly in one of her scarves and tied one end to the metal rack in her closet.

Do it. You might as well. You know what the result of the test is going to be.

Sara took a deep breath and shoved the acidic voice in her head away. She had to know if she was pregnant. Maybe, by some act of a God she doubted existed, the test would come back negative and she could continue living her life as Sara the Slut instead of Sara the Slut Who Got Herself Knocked Up.

You're ruined either way.

Sara picked up the stick and swallowed the ball bearing in her throat. She'd sneaked out of the house in the early hours of the morning the night before and walked the eight miles to Dawson, Infinity's neighboring town to the southwest, to the nearest Walmart. She had spotted no one she knew, and after circling the aisle three times, she'd snatched a home pregnancy test she'd seen advertised on television. Quickly paying for it in cash and not so much as getting a sideways glance from the definite stoner manning the register, she walked the eight miles back to Infinity, arriving home just in time to shower and change for another hellish day of school. The pregnancy test box she had stashed in the bowels of her closet.

And now, after yet another day of whispers in the hallway, vague yet incriminating Tweets and stone faces from Ashley and her former friends, Sara was holding the test and waiting for her fate to be sealed when it came back positive.

There's always suicide…

Sara took a deep breath and one last look in the mirror. She didn't even recognize the walking dead girl staring back at her.

***

SARA vomited again, this time dropping the white stick to the tile floor. It clattered a few times before landing display side up. When Sara saw the two distinct pink lines again, her stomach lurched and she emptied its contents into the toilet bowl for the third time.

Two pink lines. Just two pink lines had the ability to

change her life forever. But she had known, hadn't she? It was her punishment for her night of recklessness. She had been wrong to believe God didn't exist; he most certainly did. And he was cruel. He was malicious. He didn't play fair. She had been raped by faceless teenage boys, and now she carried the seed of one of them tucked deep inside her womb. Yes, God surely existed. And he didn't care about justice, and he wasn't compassionate. He was a dictator in the sky, a merciless, unrepentant dictator.

What am I going to do?

Sara leaned back against the tub, strings of vomit and saliva dangling from her bottom lip. The familiar voice, the one that had been assaulting her since Val's party, took up its bullhorn in her brain again.

You have no options, whore! You're better off dead and you know it!

Sara felt sobs bubble in her chest, and she let them spill out into the atmosphere unencumbered. Her parents weren't home from work yet, and even if they were, would it really matter? She'd be showing signs of pregnancy in a few short weeks, anyway. They were going to find out sooner or later. *Everyone* would find out sooner or later.

You have no options. You're destroyed now. Done.

And she didn't have options. The voice was right. What kind of life could she give a child when she herself was a child? When she didn't even know who the father was? Sara and Ashley had always scoffed at how teenage mothers seemed to be glorified by *MTV* and news organizations alike. She and Ashley had sworn off such girls as trashy and slutty; and when two girls in last year's senior class became pregnant, Sara remembered the disgust she felt for them, mixed with an overwhelming sense of superiority and relief. Those girls had become loners quickly, and both had ended up choosing to complete online courses instead of walking around with their scarlet letters pushing through their abdomens in the hallways of Infinity High School. And now Sara was the pregnant girl. She was the one who was about to become the subject of more dinner table conversations than she cared to think about.

All because you couldn't say no. All because you liked *it.*

What was left? Where was she to go from here? She couldn't keep the baby, that much she knew. How could she raise a child when she couldn't figure out how to keep *herself* out of harm's way? Putting the child up for adoption was the best option, but that meant she'd have to undergo nine months of hell and a lifetime of scrutiny. And she'd also know that somewhere in the world a part of herself was learning to tie its shoes, getting on the school bus for the first time, graduating from high school. She didn't know if she could bear to think about such things for the rest of her life.

There's still another option…

Sara's body rocked with sobs when she realized the voice was right. There *was* another option, one that could take care of her pregnancy quickly and keep at least a shred of her dignity alive. She couldn't believe she was even considering the idea of having an abortion, but the reality of the situation beat down on her, and she didn't see any other means by which to put her life in order again. She felt like a monster for even entertaining the thought. Infinity was very much a pro-life, conservative community, and Sara's whole ideology and upbringing clashed with the notion of murdering—yes, *murdering*—the child growing inside her. If it ever got out that Sara had extinguished her pregnancy, she'd surely be shunned, or worse.

You have no choice, Sara. It has to be this way.

It had to be this way. This option had to be the one that would cause the least amount of collateral damage. She couldn't waddle around Infinity High School for nine months without having all the males who had assaulted her at Val's party wondering if the bump they saw pushing through her sweater was the result of the five minutes of drunken ecstasy they'd shared—no, *taken*—from her. A swift, decisive abortion was the best way. She had no attachment to the bundle of cells growing inside her. She didn't *love* it. The child would represent her greatest failure if it should be allowed to live, and she knew she would suffocate under the weight of that realization.

Sara looked at the positive pregnancy test on the floor. The two pink lines mocked her, goaded her. But they would be easy to erase. They could be undone. All she needed was *Google* and a little time.

You're finally thinking straight, Sara.

***

SARA sat in the bathtub, the straight razor hovering over the blue veins of her left wrist. She'd heard somewhere that you wanted to slice vertically to maximize the bleed-out and to reduce the time it took to die. But, then again, she deserved a slow, agonizing death. She'd killed her baby, after all. Had made an appointment at a clinic in Toledo, had lied to her parents about going shopping, had *murdered* her child. And now she was numb. Hollowed out beyond repair. She hadn't anticipated the immediate regret she'd felt, hadn't anticipated the *mourning* she was in for the life she'd just exterminated. There was nothing left to live for. There was nothing left to hope after. She would forever be the monster who had murdered her innocent, unborn child. And she couldn't live with that. And she wouldn't.

Do it, Sara! Get it over with! Your life is over, anyway!

The voice inside her head was back, the same one that spoke in a malicious, accusing fashion. She had been afraid of it up until now, but as she practiced a few scratches on her wrist, she found herself completely agreeing with its biting accusations.

What if people find out? What if they really know what you've done? You'll be known as a whore and *a murderer!*

Sara sank deeper into the tepid bathwater. If only she could be someone else. If only she could trade places with another girl, a pure girl, a *whole* girl. If only she could relive the last two months of her life, to hit the reset button and wipe out all the things that had gotten her to this point. Two months ago she had been a Cornell hopeful with the world seemingly at her fingertips. Now, she was a murdering slut who was about to take the coward's way out.

It's hopeless because you're hopeless.

Sara swallowed hard and attempted to steady her trembling right hand. What would it feel like to open the veins underneath her skin? What would it feel like to die? And what came after?

Nothing. Oblivion. Just do it—now! You're not worth even the deliberation.

Sara knew the voice was right. She wasn't worth it, wasn't worth anythi—

YOU'RE WORTH IT.

What was this? A new voice in her head? Surely she was going insane. She should just kill herself already, if only to stop the voices from driving her crazier than she already was.

Do it, Sara. You're beyond saving now. You're beyond all hope of love.

Tears streamed down her face. She was so unlovable. So incapable of ever being loved again. No one wanted someone else's sloppy seconds, and that is what she would forever be.

DON'T DO IT. YOU ARE LOVED MORE THAN YOU KNOW.

Death is your only option.

CHOOSE LIFE, SARA.

The voices swam in her head, one malicious and accusatory, the other a strange mix of calm and serene. What was going on? For a moment, the tiniest flicker of hope ignited in her spirit. She sat up in the tub and the water beaded from her hair.

Don't listen to the other voice, Sara. Focus. Remember, you're damaged goods. You're dirty and used and unclean. Kill yourself and rid the world of the disease that is you.

YOU'RE WORTH MORE THAN YOU CAN IMAGINE.

Sara set the razor on the side of the tub and drew her knees to her chest. Her body trembled with sobs, yet her spirit had been infiltrated by an overwhelming—what was it?—*peace.*

There aren't second chances in life, Sara. You know that! Do you really think you'll ever be anything more than a murdering, worthless slut?

THERE ARE SECOND CHANCES. AND THIRD AND FOURTH CHANCES.

No! You will always be a baby killer! You'll always be the slutty girl who slept with the entire male population of Infinity High School! You can't escape that! You can't ever redeem yourself from that kind of mistake!

Sara rocked with sobs. How could she move forward? How could she ever live again if she didn't take her life now? And *why* couldn't she kill herself now? The opportunity was perfect, and she had been about to open her wrists and end it all. What was stopping her? The turmoil of it all was exhausting. *Everything* about the last two months had been exhausting.

It's not going to get better, Sara! Do you really think life will get any easier if you choose not to kill yourself now?

Sara couldn't take the vicious voice anymore. Grabbing the razor, she hurled it at the bathroom door with a scream.

You fool! You stupid, disgusting whore*!!*

Sara's chest heaved, and she leaned back in the tub and wondered if she had made a big mistake by not killing herself. Mostly, she was just bone-weary. It was all too much.

REST, SARA. BE AT PEACE.

Sara closed her eyes as the tears continued to fall in rivulets down her cheeks. Rest was what she needed. And right now the strange rekindling of hope she felt in her spirit was enough. Maybe not enough for a lifetime—maybe not enough for a week—but, for now, it was enough. She had no idea what tomorrow would bring, no idea what adversities and scrutiny the day *after* tomorrow carried. But as she cried in the bathtub, only moments away from having spared her life from the cool slice of a razorblade, she allowed the spark of hope to fan to flame.

And she rested. At least for now.

Part III
Freedom

Chapter Seven

THE ACCUSER'S LIPS PULLED back into a triumphant snarl.

"Now they know your story, Sara. What do you think they think of you? The all-American girl who got herself knocked up and then killed her baby because she got scared. It's classic, really."

Sara's eyes, now bleary with tears, sought the young man's peaceful stare. His dark eyes were still locked on hers, but now a solitary tear trickled down his cheek.

"Your family would disown you if they knew, Sara," the Accuser continued. "They would brand you a killer and demand you erase their name from yours if they truly knew what you did."

Sara felt the first tremble overtake her body. As she stood naked and exposed to the room, to the world, the familiar wave of nausea swept over her. It was the same nausea that came every time she thought of what she had done. It was the same repulsion that had made her an insomniac, had turned her into a cutter. The sweet, cool slice of the razor blade over her thighs had become a way to release some of the guilt that expanded within her and threatened to explode into suicidal thoughts and eating disorders, into bouts of depression and horrific nightmares. When crimson blood bubbled from the fresh cut, she felt she was paying a debt for her sins. Blood for blood. Lifeblood for life. But she knew all the blood flowing through her veins could never atone for what she had done. No amount of sacrifice on her part could make her blameless again.

"You killed your baby, Sara. You *murdered* your unborn child," the Accuser said as he stepped behind her. He ground the gun barrel into her temple and whispered loudly enough for the other hostages to hear.

"Do you ever wonder what that child could've become, Sara? Do you ever wonder whether the bundle of cells and the heartbeat you extinguished could've changed the world?"

Sara felt herself break. She couldn't do it. She couldn't be courageous in the face of these accusations. Because the Accuser was *right*. He was spot-on. She was a murderer. She had killed a life that had been growing inside her womb—a *child* that had been growing inside her womb. The tears rolled down her cheeks and her throat closed up. This was how she was going to die. And she deserved it.

"You eliminated a human life in the name of convenience, Sara. You justified your action by telling yourself that you'd never be able to give the child the best possible life. But, really, we both know you killed your baby out of fear and pride. Right, Sara?"

Sara tried to swallow but couldn't. Her body convulsed with sobs, and it was all she could do not to crumple to the floor.

Just kill me! Shoot me! Do it! Do it!

The young man's eyes flickered to life. Sara watched them transform in an instant. The tranquility vanished and fierceness took over. As the Accuser destroyed her with his words, Sara's only hope was in the young man's eyes. They were the only thing she had left, the only thing that kept her from surrendering to the blessed anesthetic of death.

"You are a soiled rag, Sara," the Accuser continued. "You are a stain on the canvas of humanity, one that can never be wiped clean."

The young man's eyes were fervent and alive. They pulsed with something Sara couldn't name, a nourishment that kept her hope alive. She drank it in through her tears and shame.

"What are soiled rags worth, Sara?" the Accuser asked. When Sara didn't answer, he twisted the gun so the barrel bit into her skin. "It's not a rhetorical question."

Sara's eyes dropped to the tiles, and the nausea overtook her again.

"N—nothing."

"Louder, Sara!" the Accuser demanded. "Tell the people what a worthless rag is worth."

"Nothing."

The Accuser brought his face close enough to her face that she could feel his hot breath violating her ear. "Louder, Sara. Tell them! *Tell them!*"

"Nothing!" Sara screamed into the diner. Her voice reverberated off the cinderblock walls, and back to her ears. She hated the sound of her voice. Hated the truth the Accuser was speaking, hated *herself.*

"That's a good girl, Sara. You have answered correctly. A soiled rag must be thrown onto a burn pile. It must be incinerated so it can't infect others."

Sara's eyes sought the young man's again. The nausea vanished when she found them, and she was astonished to see the anger boiling in them.

"The wages of your sin should be death, Sara," the

Accuser spewed. "You shouldn't be allowed to walk the earth with the rest of us. You took a life, and you deserve to die."

He's right! You know he's right!

"You can't stop the pain, can you? You cut yourself. You tried to party your way from the truth. You tried whoring yourself out to any man who bought you a drink. You pop more antidepressants than you can count. And, for what? You know you can't hide from the truth. No amount of alcohol, no amount of pills, no amount of sex, no amount of cutting can fix you, Sara. You are not fixable. You are worthless and vile. You are a *baby killer!*"

Sara's knees buckled, and she fell to the floor hard. Her eyes fell, and she knew she couldn't take another breath in this life. Not when she had murdered her own child. Not when she had done all the things the Accuser had said.

"It's too much, isn't it, Sara?" the Accuser said, stooping. "The guilt is too heavy. So is the realization that you can never be loved again—that you aren't worthy of love."

"Stop—please…"

"You should die today. It would be better if you did. You know it, and so does everyone else."

"P—please!"

"Please, what, Sara? Please stop holding a mirror to your rotted soul? Please stop revealing the truth about your nature?"

Stop! Just kill me!

Sara's head felt as if it might explode. She longed for the Accuser's bullet, longed for it to destroy her memory, to take away the pain.

"Who would want you, Sara? Who could ever love a *whore?* You might as well kill yourself like Abigail.

You're both murderers. But, somehow, the murder you committed seems far worse."

Sara couldn't take her eyes from the floor. She was finished. The guilt pressed upon her to the point of suffocation. She needed the Accuser's bullet—*needed* it.

"Say it loudly, Sara. Tell them you deserve to die."

Sara had nothing left but her shame. It didn't cost her anything more to admit the truth.

"I–I deserve to die."

"You can do better than that! Tell them! Let the world know you deserve to die!"

Sara took a deep breath. With everything she had within her, whatever broken pieces she had left, she screamed as loudly as she possibly could.

"I deserve to die!"

"*ENOUGH!!*"

The voice boomed over her own, as loud as thunder. She heard the Accuser's knees pop as he quickly stood. She looked up from the tiles and saw the young man standing, his blazing eyes locked on the Accuser.

"What did you say, boy?"

The young man didn't waver. His voice was strong, clear. "I said that's enough."

"Go sit over there, Sara," the Accuser said, pointing to a table to his left. "Now!"

Sara felt the life return to her extremities. Placing her palms on the floor, she pushed herself up and on shaky legs, walked over to the table, pulled out a chair, and sat down. Her heart thundered, and she couldn't believe she was alive. She knew she shouldn't be. She deserved death, and she still lusted after the Accuser's bullet. But now, a standoff was occurring, one that couldn't possibly end well for the unarmed young man.

"You have guts, I'll give you that," the Accuser said.

Sara picked up on the slight tremor in his voice immediately. The fear was back. He was unnerved.

"It's over. Now." The young man's arms rested at his sides. His stubbled face was stone, his eyes fierce and probing.

"And how do you think you'll stop me? I don't know you, but you're only one man. Unarmed. Come at me and a bullet will explode your heart."

"Let them go."

The Accuser laughed, although it did nothing to quell his uneasiness.

"You don't seem to understand. I'm trying to set them free. Worthless sinners like Sara deserve to find freedom from their oppressive iniquities."

"You know nothing of freedom," the young man said. "Freedom gives life. It doesn't bring death."

The Accuser cocked his head to the right. "Oh. So we have a philosopher in our midst, albeit a misguided one."

"The only thing misguided is your interpretation of freedom."

The Accuser studied the young man for a moment. Sara couldn't understand how he saw the young man as a potential threat. Besides being handsome in a rugged, working man's way, he was nothing to really write home about. There was no way he would be able to overpower the Accuser, even if the gun didn't skew the odds in favor of the Accuser.

"I'm done talking to you," the Accuser said dismissively. "Sit down or I'll shoot you. Sara, come here."

Sara stood obediently.

"I'll take her place," the young man said.

What?

The Accuser's eyes narrowed. "What did you say?"

The young man's jaw muscles clenched once.

"I said I'll take her place."

The Accuser grabbed Sara, pulled her close. He jammed the gun into her temple again.

"She is a worthless, vile sinner. She isn't worthy to live."

The gun dug into her skin, and the Accuser's vise grip around her neck tightened. A thousand things swam through her mind, and her pulse was almost one continuous beat. She saw the resolution in the young man's eyes.

"I'll take her place."

The Accuser's voice came out strained, forced. He was faltering. Something about the young man was getting to him.

"I'm afraid you don't understand how this works— what is your name, boy?"

"Jessie."

"Okay, *Jessie*. I don't think you understand how this works. Sara, here, must face her sins. She is a *murderer*. She is a stain on the canvas of humanity ..."

"And I will take her place," Jessie interrupted.

Sara watched the Accuser's black eyes become slits.

"She is a worthless, sub-human ..."

"And I will take her place. I will take *all* their places."

A few gasps staccato-ed the air as Jessie spread his arms to indicate all the hostages.

"I don't know you, Jessie. And if I don't know you, you have theoretically lived your entire life without sin, although the probability of that actually happening is zero. Why would you, whose transgressions I can't see, give up your life for these wretched creature?"

Jessie didn't falter or miss a beat.

"Because I believe in true freedom."

The Accuser reeled as though he'd been slapped across the face.

"What do you mean by *true freedom*? Freedom can only happen after one has stared his sin in the face, suffered under the weight of it and sacrificed himself to its shame."

Jessie's fingers folded into fists at his side.

"Your freedom is based on suffering and destruction. Mine is unconditional. I will die so they can live."

The Accuser was speechless for only the second time since the ordeal had begun. Sara felt the tug of hope rise in her chest, although the familiar oppression of her guilt rose with it.

The Accuser leveled the gun at Jessie's chest.

"And what if I shoot you right now and continue with the rest of them as if nothing has happened?"

The fear in the Accuser's voice was more pronounced than ever.

"You haven't accused me of anything."

"There's nothing to accuse!" the Accuser snapped. "You are spotless. I can't see your sin. And that's precisely what worries me. *Why* can't I recognize your transgressions? You *have* none!"

"Then give me their sins," Jessie said, softly. "Give them to me—all of them. Accuse me so they can walk out of here."

The Accuser was shaken. Sara saw him cracking and crumbling under Jessie's composed disposition. Sara knew before the Accuser what the man would do. He had to. He wasn't used to being unnerved.

"You would allow me to kill you to save them? To be clear, Jessie, you would trade your life for theirs?"

"I would. I *will*."

The Accuser took a deep breath. Let it out. He was calculating, considering. Sara knew his next words would seal the fates of everyone in the diner.

"Everyone—you have thirty seconds to exit the diner. Use the back door. If anyone contacts the authorities, you will be dead by nightfall. Move!"

Sara couldn't believe it. Her brain wouldn't allow the Accuser's words to sink in, and it took a moment for her feet to remember how to move. The remaining hostages quickly sprung to their feet and crunched glass and slipped in pools and smears of blood as they frantically made their way to the back of the diner. Sara was on her feet, ready to sprint to the hallway, when the Accuser's voice boomed into the small space.

"Not you, Sara! You'll stay here. Sit back down. The fun is only starting."

Chapter Eight

SARA'S BLOOD BOOMED IN HER temples as she watched the last of the hostages disappear down the hallway that led to freedom. She knew now beyond a shadow of a doubt that she would never be joining them. She would die here. Jessie couldn't save her, not against the Accuser's gun, and dying in her place wasn't going to be a reality. Otherwise she would be outside the diner like the other hostages. It would all be over in a matter of moments. And there was nothing she could do to stop it.

The Accuser turned to Sara but kept his gun trained on Jessie.

"Thanks for staying, Sara. I can't wait to see how this turns out. Don't you feel like a damsel in distress about now?" He nodded at Jessie. "Your hero's here to save you." He laughed. "A hero to save a murdering whore. Even Shakespeare couldn't have written it better."

"I'll die in her place," Jessie said, his hands at his sides, his dark eyes unwavering. "Let her go."

"And what fun would that be?" the Accuser said, stepping closer to Jessie. "What fun would it be for Sara to be let go without seeing you suffer?"

Sara couldn't bear it. No one should die for her. She was dirty, useless, worthless. She was everything the Accuser had called her, everything and more. Why would Jessie—a complete stranger—even care about her miserable life, anyway?

I'm not worth it, Jessie. Save yourself.

Sara heard her voice before she realized she had even spoken.

"P—please. Let Jessie go. He doesn't deserve to die for me. He doesn't even know me, and …"

"I'll take her place," Jessie said, calmly.

The Accuser's smile dripped with mockery. "Jessie, listen to the whore! You have no stains that I can see; therefore you are theoretically sinless, even though I am certain you are as filthy as the rest of them. Why would you give your life away for damaged goods?"

Jessie's milk chocolate eyes found Sara's. She immediately dropped hers to the floor in shame.

"There's no such thing as damaged goods."

The Accuser sneered. "And what is this woman standing here? Is she not a baby-killer? Was her womb not a crime scene? There *is* such a thing as damaged goods, boy, and she is standing here unworthy to breathe the same air as you."

Sara felt her knees give out. She collapsed to the tiles, her legs unable to hold her iniquity-riddled body. The Accuser's words pierced her heart. She was worthy of death and nothing more. She had been about to sprint from the diner and allow an innocent man to die for her when she was the one unworthy of life itself.

"I will die in her place," Jessie said again.

The Accuser's eyes narrowed, and his voice became deadly. "You're mocking me."

Jessie didn't flinch. "I'm not mocking you."

Sara barely saw the Accuser's fist smash against Jessie's face. The swiftness with which the older man had moved was almost unbelievable. Jessie staggered, fell to one knee for a moment. Blood poured from a nasty gash on his cheek as he slowly got back to his feet.

"Jessie!" Sara cried out.

Stop! Stay down!

The Accuser walked a slow circle around Jessie, eyes predatory and vicious.

"Tell me, Jessie, what is your greatest sin? I can't see it, but it must be locked away inside of you."

Jessie said nothing. The young man's eyes were locked on Sara's, and the wave of shame she had felt now came back tenfold. She wanted to stand up, wanted to get to her feet, but it seemed right for her to stay on the floor. She was the lowest of the low, the most vile creature in the room. The floor was suitable for her.

"I asked you a question, boy! What is your greatest sin?"

Jessie stood stone-still, his arms at his sides. His eyes were both tremendously unnerving and deeply peaceful as he seemed to search Sara's soul.

Say something, Jessie!

The Accuser stopped walking, now stood in front of Jessie.

"Why is it you don't answer me? Are you afraid of the secrets of your soul? Are you scared of the truth, boy?"

"It's the truth that brings freedom," Jessie answered, his voice calm.

The Accuser scoffed. "What *is* truth, Jessie?"

Jessie said nothing and the Accuser laughed mockingly. "The only truth I see is the truth I'm standing in. You are here. I win, and you lose. Even though I can't see your stains, you are as flawed as Sara. I am only going to ask one more time, Jessie. What is your greatest sin?"

Jessie took a deep breath and exhaled calmly. The Accuser flipped the gun in his hand. Sara realized what was going to happen as the Accuser raised his arm.

"No! Don't!"

In a flash the Accuser slashed the gun across Jessie's forehead. Sara heard the sickening thud of metal on flesh and bone as Jessie fell to the floor, blood bursting from a deep slash above his right eye.

He didn't even raise his arms to protect himself!

Jessie rolled onto his stomach, and blood poured onto the tiles. Sara's eyes blurred with tears, but she didn't dare go to him.

"When I ask a question, you answer it!" the Accuser boomed into the empty diner.

Jessie placed his palms on the floor and tried to push himself to his feet. He collapsed under the weight of himself, the blow to his head certainly disorienting him. Sara found it miraculous that he hadn't been knocked out.

"Get up! I'm not finished with you!" The Accuser's foot lashed out and met Jessie's ribcage. The young man groaned as his breath left his lungs.

"Get up!" The Accuser kicked him again, and a third time. Sara cried out for him to stop, but it was no use. The Accuser's foot continued to slam into Jessie's ribs and stomach, and the young man instinctively curled into the fetal position to ward off further blows.

"Do you think you can mock me and get away with it?" the Accuser roared, clearly winded. "Get up!" He delivered one more vicious kick that caught Jessie under the chin. Jessie's head snapped back and the blood streaming from his forehead beaded into the air and splattered the tiles three feet away.

Sara rocked on the floor, hugging herself tightly. She couldn't let Jessie take these beatings for her, couldn't let an innocent man undergo so much torture for her sake. Every blow the Accuser landed felt like a sucker punch to her own gut.

"Get up! Now!"

Jessie slowly rolled onto his stomach and placed his palms on the tiles.

No! Stay down! If you get up, he'll kill you!

But the young man didn't heed Sara's silent pleas. Instead, he pushed himself to his knees and then to his feet. Swaying a little, he turned his head to the side and spit out a stream of bright red blood. The Accuser sneered.

"Is it worth it? Is *she* worth it? You don't even know her."

Jessie's voice came out strained but sure. "I'll die for her."

The Accuser looked at Sara and shook his head.

"I don't see it, Jessie. I don't see why you would give up breathing for her sake. If you aren't going to tell me your darkest sin, at least answer me this: why?"

Jessie didn't hesitate. "Because I love her."

Jessie's words floored Sara.

Love? He loves *me!?*

There was no chance Jessie could love her. Aside from the fact that he'd never met her before, she was everything the Accuser accused her of being—and more. How could someone—a complete stranger—stare death in the face and claim love for someone he'd never met? It made no sense at all. And yet...

And yet Sara felt her heart swell with his words. A feeling of lightness, of weightlessness, of giddiness settled over her body. For a moment, she had the irrational feelings of a middle school girl who'd seen her crush walk by. But, at the same time, the feeling was different. She couldn't explain it, but the feeling was a mixture of hope and serenity, of peace and—

Freedom...

Could it be? Was it possible for her to feel the first rumblings of freedom from the words of a complete stranger? She yearned to hear him speak the words again, yearned for him to say the three words that had melted her heart and given her the first inclinations of purpose. It was as if his three simple words had ripped out some of the Accuser's fiery darts.

But—how? Why?

The Accuser threw his head back and laughed.

"You *love* her? Are you serious, Jessie? You *love* her? Did I hit your head too hard, or something? You *love* her? You don't even *know* her."

Jessie looked at Sara again. And when his eyes met hers, Sara was hit with the realization that, just as she knew the Accuser's voice from somewhere, she also knew Jessie's. As illogical and improbable as it seemed, she had heard Jessie's voice before. Somewhere, some place, some time.

I've heard his voice before. But where?

"I love her," Jessie repeated. "And I will die for her."

The familiarity of his voice was almost too much for Sara. Her brain searched her past for any clue as to when and under what circumstances she had heard Jessie speak.

"You're worth it."

Sara gasped.

It can't be...

"You are insane, son," the Accuser said, but Sara barely heard him.

"DON'T DO IT. YOU ARE LOVED MORE THAN YOU KNOW."

Sara swallowed, fighting back new tears.

"CHOOSE LIFE, SARA."

"She's not even worth the body bag she'll end up in when I'm finished here," the Accuser continued, his voice drowned out by the one—*Jessie's*—from her past.

"YOU'RE WORTH MORE THAN YOU CAN IMAGINE."

"She's broken, Jessie! She can't be fixed! You can't save someone who isn't capable of being saved!"

"THERE ARE SECOND CHANCES, SARA. THERE ARE THIRD AND FOURTH CHANCES..."

"Her whole life had been chaos! She'll never be content,

boy! Because restless whores can't find contentment!"

"REST, SARA. BE AT PEACE."

Sara's heart felt as if it might burst. Jessie loved her. He knew her in a mysterious way, one Sara couldn't yet comprehend but desperately wanted to. As strange as it seemed, his love was what she craved. She couldn't let him die in his innocence. Even if it meant her life would be extinguished, at least she would die knowing she was loved deeply.

"Stop!" Sara screamed. She stood, her legs now steady, her feet now firm.

The Accuser pivoted and aimed the gun at her head, never taking his eyes off Jessie.

"What was that, Sara? You want me to stop? I'm just having a conversation with Jessie."

"Leave him alone. He hasn't done anything wrong. I'm the one who's guilty."

The Accuser's mocking smile was back. "Impressive of you, Sara. Very impressive. You are guilty, and you do deserve to die. But, I'm afraid you're too late. Jessie, here, has offered to take your place. And, to tell you the truth, I can't wait to make him feel pain."

"I'll die for her," Jessie said. The resolution in his voice, the *love* that exuded from his four simple words, drove a stake through Sara's heart. He couldn't die for her. He was too good and she was too filthy.

"Please—let him go," Sara pleaded, her voice breaking.

"It's too late, Sara," the Accuser said. He quickly pivoted and aimed the gun at Jessie's midsection. Jessie didn't even flinch.

"No!" Sara screamed. But her voice was drowned out by the deafening boom of the Accuser's gun.

Chapter Nine

JESSIE STUMBLED BACKWARD AND clutched his right side. A stream of blood seeped through his fingers, and he blindly sought the table behind him. Finding it, he sat down as the blood continued to flow at an alarming rate. The shot had hit him under the ribcage, and Sara knew that even if the bullet hadn't torn through vital organs, the blood loss would soon render him unconscious before killing him.

"That was your bullet, Sara. Make sure you take in all the blood. The way he's grimacing with each breath. It's all your fault."

Sara tried to go to Jessie, but the Accuser blocked her way.

"You better stay where you are, Sara. Things could get messy."

The Accuser slowly walked to the table where Jessie sat clutching his side.

"Now do I have your attention, boy? Now do I get your cooperation?"

"Please—stop! He's bleeding! He needs a doctor!"

Sara was nothing more than a helpless bystander. The Accuser was going to murder an innocent man, and she could do absolutely nothing about it.

The Accuser swung the gun around. "Not another word

from you! Anything else and I put a bullet through his brain!"

Sara could do nothing but whimper where she stood. Already, Jessie's face had gone ashen with blood loss.

He's going to die—and there's nothing I can do about it!

"I'm going to ask you again, Jessie," the Accuser said, pointing the gun back at Jessie's head. "I'm going to ask you about your secret sin. What is the one thing you're hiding that no one knows about?"

Jessie looked him in the eye and then turned his head to Sara. His dark eyes were physically weaker, but they conveyed more life than ever.

"Nothing? You sit here bleeding to death and you won't answer my question? Who are you, boy?"

The Accuser pointed the gun at Jessie's hand clutching to the tabletop and pulled the trigger. Jessie screamed in agony as a bullet tore a hole through the bones, tendons and flesh of his left hand.

"See what happens when you don't cooperate?"

Jessie fell from the tabletop onto the floor. The table tipped over and fell onto his chest, and Jessie cried out as it cracked against his sternum. The Accuser quickly kicked the table away. Sara was reduced to nothing more than a sobbing mess.

"I'll ask again," the Accuser said, standing over Jessie. The young man writhed in pain as blood poured from his side and hand.

"What is your greatest sin, Jessie? Answer me!"

But Jessie looked past him into Sara's eyes. It seemed to take everything within him, but he lifted his head from the tiles and locked eyes with Sara—the worthless woman he had called his beloved.

The Accuser aimed and fired a shot through Jessie's right foot. Instantly his white sneaker bloomed with dark blood, and Sara knew that if somehow she lived through this experience, she'd hear his cries of agony in her dreams.

"And, now? Come on, Jessie! Answer me!"

The Accuser wasted no time in firing another shot, this one through Jessie's left foot.

Sara collapsed in her own agony. This was *her* fault! Jessie was being tortured because of *her*! After his voice had kept her alive all those years ago, after he had stopped her from slicing her wrists with a razorblade, she was watching him die—for *her*.

"Had enough, boy?"

The Accuser kicked Jessie's right elbow. The young man's hand fell away from the seeping wound at his side. Blood poured from the hole, and Sara knew Jessie needed immediate medical attention if he had any chance of living to see the next hour. But just as she knew Jessie's wounds needed prompt tending, she also knew this whole ordeal was going to end with both of them dead.

The Accuser aimed the gun and fired a shot through Jessie's right hand.

"You are dying for a *whore*!"

Jessie's hands and feet leaked blood as Sara watched the Accuser kick Jessie in the side. Jessie's cries of pain assaulted Sara's ears, because they were supposed to be *her* cries of pain. She was supposed to die, not Jessie.

The Accuser stooped and smacked Jessie on the face to get his attention.

"You said you would die for them all. You aren't just dying for Sara, the murdering whore. You are dying for a rapist and an adulterer. You are dying for a liar, a thief and a roomful of hypocrites. There are no saints among them, Jessie. They are all vermin worthy of extermination. And you are choosing to give up your life for them. And for what? Because you *love* them as you supposedly love Sara? Because you feel some sort of guilt for a past transgression, and now you are trying to atone for it?"

Jessie raised his head, his neck muscles trembling. He coughed once and fought for the air required for his next statement.

"It's—it's for freedom. For love."

The Accuser sneered. "Love. Right. No, you are dying because you are stupid enough to believe the people you claim to set free would reciprocate. You're ignorant enough to believe that perhaps those pitiful excuses for human beings could actually love you back."

Jessie said nothing and the Accuser laughed.

"How heroic. How pathetically heroic."

The Accuser spat in Jessie's face before standing. "Unfortunately, one simply can't die for a horde of sinners and expect them to be free. There is no precedent for it."

Jessie lifted his head a little. "It's love."

"Based on what? Love is conditional. It's temporary. It ends."

Sara watched Jessie struggle to keep his head off the floor.

"M—mine doesn't."

The Accuser laughed. "Your love doesn't end? When I put a bullet through your heart, your body will shut down. You will die, and your love will end. There's no such thing as infinite love."

But even as the Accuser spoke against the reality of infinite love, Sara knew it existed. Somehow, and in some way, she believed Jessie exhibited the traits of such love, that he could *extend* such love. But how? Who was Jessie? And what did his love matter if he ended up dying for it?

"M—my love is unconditional. It's—it's permanent."

The Accuser's mocking smile flickered. Sara picked up on it right away.

He's scared again. He's afraid Jessie might be right.

"You can't claim infinite love unless you yourself are an infinite being. And you can't die for a host of sinners unless you

106

yourself are sinless," the Accuser said. He squinted his eyes, but Sara still caught the small tremble of his voice.

Jessie said nothing as he gasped for breath.

The Accuser turned to Sara. "What do you think, Sara? Can a dead man love after he's dead?" He aimed the gun at Jessie's chest.

"What do you think, Sara? Is he immortal? Is he not bleeding all over these tiles?"

Sara knew she had to say something, but everything she wanted to say seemed so futile.

"I—please! He needs a doctor!"

"Dead men don't need doctors!" the Accuser shouted.

Jessie lifted his head again. His eyes found Sara's. What she saw wasn't fear in the face of death, or even the pain that was wracking his body. No, she saw something greater, something more transcendent. She saw peace and …

Freedom.

With one last gasp, Jessie spoke.

"It's done."

And then the Accuser pulled the trigger.

Chapter Ten

THE ACCUSER ROARED IN TRIUMPH as Sara ran to Jessie's lifeless body. She didn't care about her own safety anymore. Her own preservation paled in comparison to Jessie's. He needed a doctor, he needed fresh blood pumped into his veins, he needed a miracle.

"Jessie!" Sara said. She put her ear to his mouth, felt no hot breath against her cheek. She checked his pulse, felt nothing.

"Dead, Sara. So much for love," the Accuser gloated.

No! He can't be dead!

Sara quickly tilted Jessie's neck back and checked for breath one last time before starting compressions. She had been certified in CPR last summer after taking classes at the YMCA, but she had never thought she'd actually have to apply what she had learned. Her brain was in such a fog she wondered if she even remembered how to do it correctly.

"Give it up, Sara," the Accuser said, touching her shoulder. She shrugged him off, repulsed at his touch. She knew that at any second he might fire a bullet through her brain and end her life, but she didn't care. Jessie was her sole purpose for living. She needed him. She *loved* him.

Come on, Jessie! Come on!

"He's dead, Sara," the Accuser said. "I hope you never really believed he could save you."

"Shut up!" Sara screamed into the diner. Tears streamed down her cheeks as she fervently compressed Jessie's chest.

"It's a pity, really," the Accuser said, circling Jessie's body so he could stand in front of Sara. "Your hero couldn't bring you freedom, could he? He'll be carried out of here in a body bag, after all. Just like you."

"Shut up!" Sara screamed again. She felt as though she teetered on the edge of delirium. The Accuser's voice—his *familiar* voice—had been terrorizing her for years. He had been in every accusation of failure, in every suicidal thought. He had told her she was worthless, that she couldn't, and shouldn't, be loved after she had aborted her child. He had plagued her, had destroyed her, had humiliated her, for years. And now she wanted to be free from him.

"Calm yourself, whore," the Accuser said. "You know you can't silence me. After all these years, I've become your friend. I'm a part of you, Sara, whether or not you want to admit it."

"You're a monster!" Sara shouted, continuing compressions. Sweat poured from her forehead and her arms were becoming weak. Still, she pressed on.

"It takes one to know one, isn't that the expression? Aren't you a monster in your own right? Not only did you murder your unborn child, but you also made a few pathetic attempts at taking your *own* life. Can you be any more selfish, Sara? Can you be any more of a *monster*?"

Sara didn't respond. She couldn't. What could she say? She knew he was right. She knew she was just as much a monster as he was. But Jessie hadn't seen her that way. Jessie had spoken through her shame, had found her beautiful despite the ugliness she felt. But now Jessie was gone and she was left with her monstrous self. All her hope had died when the Accuser had put the bullet through Jessie's heart.

"Stop trying to revive him, Sara. He's dead. He's not coming back."

"Shut up!"

"He was a fake. A phony. He disappointed you as you disappoint yourself."

"Get away from …"

The Accuser stooped over Jessie's body. When Sara looked up, the Accuser's face was no more than a foot from her own. His eyes were dancing with sick triumph. His devilish smirk mocked her. He pressed the gun into her forehead. He would pull the trigger and it would all be over.

"There's one thing you need to remember, whore. I always win."

A loud boom shook the diner. For a terrifying moment, Sara thought the Accuser had shot her. But when she felt the ground vibrating under her knees, she knew she was still very much alive.

"What are you doing?" the Accuser shouted over the rumbling that was gaining both in decibels and in strength. Sara saw the fear in his dark eyes as he fell backward as the ground began to shake.

This can't be happening! I can't do compressions anymore!

Sara's hands fell away from Jessie's chest as the ground beneath her trembled. The violence of the earthquake grew in intensity, and tables and chairs toppled and glasses from the waitress station's shelves fell to the floor and shattered. She quickly crawled to the waitress station and held on.

After all of this—an earthquake is how I'm going to die!

The Accuser attempted to push himself to his feet, but the earthquake threw him back onto the tiles. His gun flew from his hand and bounced with the vibrations of the ground to the south wall of the diner.

I need to get the gun!

But any thoughts Sara had about letting go of the waitress station to make an attempt to procure the weapon vanished when the ground began to crumble. Tiles burst and the middle of the diner ripped open into a chasm, that divided east and west. Jessie's body, bloodied and buffeted by the earthquake was on one side of the gash, and the Accuser was on the other, frantically trying to grab onto the legs of a bouncing table. The room split from the middle outward, and Sara realized with horror that the waitress station would be consumed by the chasm. She needed to make a decision, and make one quickly. She looked at Jessie's body, considered the back exit of the diner, and leapt to her left a few seconds before the waitress station vanished into the chasm. She landed hard on her left side and banged the back of her head against a toppled table. On the other side of the chasm, the Accuser frantically clawed at the ground. It didn't take long for Sara to realize the reason for the Accuser's terror.

The front of the diner is tilting—it's tilting toward the chasm!

All at once, the glass front door of the diner burst open, and bright morning light filled the darkness of the small room. Sara heard a clatter from the back hallway, and when she looked behind her, morning light streamed from the now open back door.

Freedom!

"No! No!"

The Accuser pawed at the ground as the front of the diner lifted from the earth. Tables and chairs fell into the gash as the forty-five degree angle of the diner floor allowed the yawn to consume once stationary objects.

"No—please! No!"

The Accuser's screams were animalistic as he began to slip toward the chasm.

"Whore! You did this! *He* did this!"

Sara watched as the Accuser lost his grip on the tiles and slid into the chasm. For a moment, his fingertips clung to the chasm's edge, but another violent tremor shook him free.

"No! No!"

The Accuser—*her* Accuser—disappeared into the chasm as the ground continued to shake.

Yes! Yes!

Sara looked at Jessie's body as the rumbling earth bounced it off the tiles.

I have to go to him! I have to save him!

Even though she knew it was irrational, and even though she knew traversing the diner to get to Jessie's body was hazardous, she had to be with him. She had to try to revive him. He loved her—and she loved him.

Tentatively crawling forward, Sara began the trek across the diner. Jessie was a little more than twenty feet away, but the violent shaking of the earth made it seem like a mile. She fell onto her face twice, but managed to pick herself up and continue crawling to him. He was all she had left. She couldn't stand on her own, couldn't find her footing in a world that shifted beneath her, so she would crawl to him.

Almost there—keep going.

Shards of broken glass bit into her knees and palms, but she continued on. Her strength was faltering and her vision was cloudy with tears, but she persisted.

Just a few more feet—almost there!

She was so close—two arm-lengths away—when something crashed against the back of her head. Her arms collapsed from underneath her, and the world spun before her eyes. She felt herself dipping into unconsciousness and fought against the impending darkness.

No! Not now! I'm so close! I'm so...

She reached for him as the blackness overtook her. She felt weightless, she felt tired.

She felt nothing.

Chapter Eleven

"WAKE UP, SARA..."

Sara felt like a helium balloon riding the air. Jessie's voice called to her from somewhere so close yet so far away.

"Wake up, Sara..."

She didn't know whether she was alive or dead. All she knew was that she wanted—no, *needed*—to go to Jessie, to find him, to tell him she loved him and hear him say he loved her.

"Wake up, Sara..."

His voice had been with her during her darkest hours. When the Accuser's barbing words had driven her to attempt suicide, Jessie's voice had stopped her. Jessie had saved her from death. He had said he loved her, and now she wanted desperately to go to him.

"Wake up, Sara..."

But she didn't want to wake up. Here, somewhere between life and death, Jessie still lived. When she awoke from whatever dream she was having, Jessie would be dead on the diner floor. Couldn't she stay here awhile longer?

"Wake up, Sara..."

Sara saw a sliver of light pierce the darkness.

"Wake up, Sara..."

The sliver grew until full, brilliant light made her squint against its newness. A silhouette looked down on her and, for a moment, Sara thought she was on an operating table in some nameless hospital.

"Wake up, Sara."

Sara's heart fluttered. The voice sounded like Jessie's, but it couldn't be. Jessie had been killed, shot dead by the Accuser.

"Hello, Sara."

Where am I?

The silhouette shifted slightly. Sara's breath caught in her throat.

It can't be!

"Jessie!?"

Jessie laughed. "It's me, Sara."

Sara pushed herself from the floor, barely feeling the thundering headache that boomed in her skull. She touched his face, felt the stubble, the warmth of his cheek.

"But—how did you …"

"Be careful, Sara," Jessie said, holding her hand. "Don't move too quickly. You were unconscious for a little bit. A table fell on your head."

This isn't making sense—how—what?!

"I—I need to stand up," Sara said.

"Okay, but slowly." Jessie helped pull Sara to her feet, and for a moment the room spun. When she looked at Jessie again, his smile was full, his eyes dancing.

"Jessie—what happened? I saw him shoot you! I felt your pulse—you weren't breathing."

"All in good time. Right now, let's make sure you're okay."

"I—I'm okay, really. I just have a headache—what happened to the chasm?"

Sara was dumbfounded when she looked around the diner. The wide chasm that had swallowed the Accuser had closed, and the front half of the diner's floor had flattened and was flush with the half Sara and Jessie stood upon. The diner floor was still scattered with broken glass and upturned tables, and the waitress station was gone. Pools and streaks of blood still marked the places where the Accuser had killed in the name of his evil freedom. When she looked at Jessie again, she realized for the first time that his wounds had closed and were no longer seeping blood. His hoodie bore no blood blossom where he had been shot below the ribcage. The wound on his forehead had closed, and if Sara hadn't seen the Accuser hit him, she never would've known Jessie's face had been marred.

"Oh!"

Sara didn't mean to gasp when she saw his hands. Jessie held them up so she could see the scarred bullet holes in them. Sara was astounded to realize that she could see *through* the holes the bullets had made.

Jessie laughed. "Don't be scared. They'll make a great conversation piece for us."

Sara looked at his shoes. The blood had vanished, and the holes—at least on his shoes—had been repaired.

Repaired? Is that even the right word?

"W—what about your feet?"

"Same as the hands." Jessie laughed again.

"Jessie—wait a minute. I can't seem to catch up. How did you live through—how are you *alive*?"

Jessie extended his hand to Sara. "I'd love to tell you the story. Come walk with me."

Sara didn't hesitate. Being with Jessie felt so right, so *freeing*. When he looked at her, he wasn't seeing all her past mistakes. He was looking at *her*. And when she looked at him, she forgot everything that had come before. He had beaten the Accuser, had silenced the monster. For that, Sara knew she could never repay him.

Sara took Jessie's hand, and the two walked through the ruins of the diner toward the front door. Jessie's hand felt so strong, his stride so sure, as he led her through the open door and into the morning light of freedom.

Part IV
Dream

Chapter Twelve

THE PERSISTENT SHRIEK OF THE alarm woke Sara from a deep sleep.

Jessie...

She was walking with him, hand-in-hand, through the streets of Lewiston. He was talking to her, explaining what had transpired at the diner, how he had been killed and then had come back to life again. His voice was so soothing, so intimate, so inviting.

Jessie...

He was telling her about freedom—*true* freedom. A freedom much different from the kind the Accuser had offered. But now it was all slipping away as her alarm clock blared into her small bedroom.

Wait—it was all a dream?

Sara clenched her eyes shut, willed sleep to find her again. The slow realization that Jessie had been nothing more than a figment of her imagination was a sucker punch to her gut. She felt like weeping. Where was she to go from here? What was she to do? For a few brief hours of sleep, Jessie had been real, and she had felt hope and new life surge into the core of her being. She still felt it now, but it was waning, receding like a tide being sucked back into the ocean. If Jessie wasn't real, and if he hadn't spoken to the shattered pieces of her soul and put them back together again, then was life still worth living? Was it worth getting out of bed and driving to the diner? She was still a fraud, still a worthless sinner. She was still a *murderer*.

I can't do it! Not without Jessie!

Tears flowed from her cheeks and she finally slammed the button on her alarm to make it stop screaming. Suddenly her tiny bedroom in her tiny apartment was silent. Too silent. If Jessie wasn't real—if he wasn't here to be her comfort, she didn't want to live anymore.

I can't go on! Not like this!

Reality was back, and it was mean—cruel. The sinking feeling in her chest as she sat up in her bed, the realization that she would have to slog on for days—weeks—months—years—as a zombie of a woman, was too much. Jessie had provided her an out from the torment that had been boiling in the cauldron of her soul since she had made the decisions that had forever altered the course of her life. Now, all she had was the diner and school. There was nothing else. Her life was a long, slow ride to nowhere.

Sara ran her hand through her hair and allowed herself a few more moments to cry the miserable, self-loathing tears that had become her norm before she picked up the shattered pieces of herself and got ready for work.

***

THE diner was unusually busy this morning, and Janice was even more cantankerous than usual. The big woman had snapped at Sara the moment Sara had walked through the door. Now, as she watched Janice berate one of the cooks for adding peppers to an omelet when the order slip had *clearly said* no peppers, Sara couldn't help but think of her dream and how Janice had heaved and clutched her chest before the Accuser had shot her.

The dream. It had been so real that walking into the diner this morning had brought with it a flood of emotions ranging from revulsion, terror, to even the swelling of hope. But the feeling of hope had been quickly dashed when Sara remembered she *had* no hope. Jessie had merely been a figment of her imagination. He wasn't real. There was no such thing as freedom, at least for her. The only thing real about her dream had been the Accuser's biting words concerning her. She truly was worthless. Truly was soiled. Truly was a *murderer.*

"Hey! Earth to Sara!" Janice snapped her fingers in Sara's face, breaking Sara's momentary trance. The big woman's face was stained with greasy sweat, and the red bandana she wore failed to keep her frizzy, live-wire bangs from fraying into the atmosphere.

"I'm not paying you to be part of the décor." Janice shoved a carafe of coffee into Sara's stomach. "You have a loner in booth thirty-six. Don't recognize him."

Sara took the carafe and her heart fluttered for a moment.

Booth thirty-six. That was the Accuser's booth.

Sara shook the ridiculous thought away and mumbled a sorry and a thank you. Before she stepped out of Sara's way, Janice squinted and snorted.

"You look terrible today, Sara. Some makeup and a good night's sleep would go a long way."

Sara bit back a comeback. She was too defeated to come up with a good one, anyway. Too tired.

If only you knew…

Sara made sure her order pad and ballpoint pen were tucked away in her apron's pouch before she made her way to the front of the diner. Her heart pounded, and Sara scolded herself for being foolish.

It was only a dream. Get over it.

But when she approached booth thirty-six, she nearly dropped the coffee carafe.

It can't be...

The man was sitting exactly where the Accuser had been sitting in her dream. Except the man wasn't the Accuser. Not even close.

I can't believe it...

The man's head was down as he studied the paper fold-up breakfast menu. But there was no mistaking his acorn hair and his hoodie. As Sara got closer, she saw the stubble on his cheeks and the lean, working-man's muscles of his forearms beneath his rolled-up sleeves. The carafe trembled in Sara's hand, and her breath caught in her throat.

"Jessie?"

She hadn't meant to say his name out loud, but the hope in her heart was too much to keep contained.

The man looked up from the menu. He wasn't Jessie.

Sara looked away, embarrassed.

"I—I—I'm sorry. I thought you were—I thought you were someone else."

The man laughed, and when Sara looked at him again, he was smiling. Her breath caught in her throat again.

He's not Jessie, but his eyes—they're—familiar.

They were a captivating olive green. And deep. So, so, deep and transcendent. Any disappointment Sara had that the man in booth thirty-six wasn't Jessie immediately vanished. Hope swirled in her chest and a lightness overtook her entire being. This man wasn't Jessie, but Sara knew beyond a shadow of a doubt that something was happening, that something was *about* to happen.

"Hello, Sara," the man said, still smiling.

His voice...

His voice was so familiar it felt like her own. She'd heard it before, felt it before, only she'd never realized its significance until now. It was this man's voice which had soothed her, calmed her fears and kept her from harming herself. It was this man's voice which had silenced the Accuser's. It was this man's voice which would bring her …

Freedom.

Sara didn't know what to say, but part of her realized she didn't need to say anything. She needed no justification for being herself, she needed no fancy words to impress the man.

"I—can I—may I sit down?"

The man-who-wasn't Jessie's smile widened further, and his olive eyes danced.

"I was hoping you'd ask to sit."

Sara untied her apron as the man extended his arm toward the booth bench across from him.

That's when Sara saw the scar on his hand.

Then I heard a loud voice in heaven say: "Now have come the salvation and the power and the kingdom of our God, and the authority of his Christ. For the accuser of our brothers, who accuses them before our God day and night, has been hurled down."

Revelation 12:10 (NIV)

About the Author

Josh Clark is an English teacher in Ohio. He is currently working on his next project.

Acknowledgements

I'd like to thank the following individuals for their unwavering support and encouragement:

Cindy: I love you more every day. Thank you for being an amazing wife and a wonderful mother. Without you, none of this would be possible. Your selflessness and sacrifice is extraordinary. I love you times infinity.

Landon Elijah and Lydia Jane: I never knew it, but every story of redemption, every book I've ever written, has been for you. You are the best gifts I've ever received, and I am blessed to be your daddy. I love you high as the sky, and low as your toes.

Mary Mueller: Thank you for always saying what you mean and meaning what you say. The time you've invested into helping me craft my writing can never be repaid. Thank you for being a great friend and mentor.

Skip Coryell: Thank you, once again, for taking a chance on me. You are a great friend and an even better man.

Ron Bell: You nailed it again. Thanks for the fantastic cover design.

And to **Jesus Christ**, Who defeated the Accuser by bringing freedom to the captives: Thank you. May the words I write only manifest Your renown.

Books By Josh Clark

The McGurney Chronicles Series
The Legend of Paul McGurney
Devil's Playground
Infinity
The Ends of the Earth

The Dakota Lester Series
Dakota Divided
Dakota Defined
Dakota Denied

Other Books
Accuser

Pregnant, unmarried and all alone. Noelle's journey will take you through the brokenness that comes as she walks out the consequences of the choices she made. Watch and see the goodness of God. Even when she didn't give Him a thought, He was still loving her and making a way. Experience God's master plan for their lives. See how He intricately knits them together and brings Noelle into a closer understanding of who He is.

Order now at amazon.com

Back in the old West, women were a rare and trea-
sured item, especially women as beautiful as Joe
Clément's young bride Jenny, with her slender fi
gure, striking red hair and pleasant disposition. So
when Joe is ambushed and his wife is abducted, this
seasoned gun fighter will stop at nothing to get her
back.

Order now at amazon.com

Suddenly, the lights went out, not just in one town or village, but all across the world. It was an act of cyber terrorism that plunged the world into the heart of darkness, into the 1000-year night, letting loose the demons of a billion souls, pitting dark against light, causing each person everywhere to choose sides. Not since Stephen King's "The Stand" has there been an apocalyptic thriller of such epic proportions. Read book one of this 5-book series and see what happens when society's thin veneer of civility is stripped away. "The God Virus" is gripping, seething and oozing with the best and worst humanity has to offer.

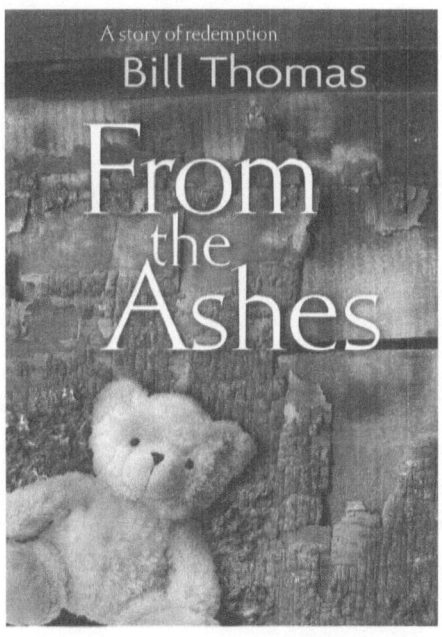

A story of redemption
Bill Thomas

From the Ashes

For Jerold, the secret came to him in the form of a mysterious text message that read simply "Help me." Frustrated and desperate, Jerold followed the clues back to his estranged Kentucky home town where the past quickly revealed itself. But things are seldom as they seem, and soon Jerold was floundering in the ashes of his tortured past from which he'd so ardently fled. Read this exciting, fast-moving thriller and grow with Jerold as he learns that pain and forgiveness are but two sides of the same coin; that the past cannot be buried and . . . The secret will not be denied.